Amos Smith 王正文 著

圖像
速學英語時態
Learn tenses in English
through pictures

商務印書館

圖像速學英語時態

作　　者：Amos Smith　王正文

責任編輯：黃家麗　郭肇敏

插　　圖：Candy Lai

出　　版：商務印書館（香港）有限公司

　　　　　香港筲箕灣耀興道 3 號東滙廣場 8 樓

　　　　　http://www.commercialpress.com.hk

發　　行：香港聯合書刊物流有限公司

　　　　　香港新界大埔汀麗路 36 號中華商務印刷大廈 3 字樓

印　　刷：美雅印刷製本有限公司

　　　　　九龍官塘榮業街 6 號海濱工業大廈 4 樓 A 室

版　　次：2016 年 3 月第 1 版第 6 次印刷

　　　　　© 2011 商務印書館（香港）有限公司

　　　　　ISBN 978 962 07 1948 6

　　　　　Printed in Hong Kong

目錄
CONTENTS

時態總圖表 TIMELINE FOR TENSES

Simple Present

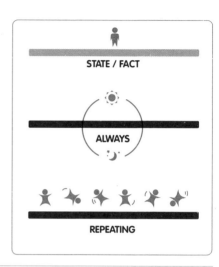

STATE / FACT

ALWAYS

REPEATING

Present Continuous

PAST   NOW   FUTURE

Simple Past

PAST   NOW   FUTURE

Past Continuous

PAST   NOW   FUTURE

Present Perfect

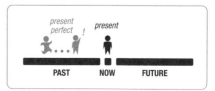

present perfect !   present

PAST   NOW   FUTURE

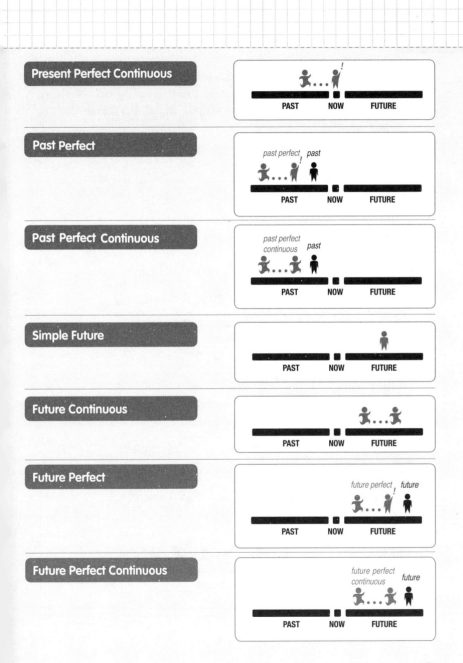

Present Perfect Continuous

PAST　NOW　FUTURE

Past Perfect

past perfect past

PAST　NOW　FUTURE

Past Perfect Continuous

past perfect continuous past

PAST　NOW　FUTURE

Simple Future

PAST　NOW　FUTURE

Future Continuous

PAST　NOW　FUTURE

Future Perfect

future perfect future

PAST　NOW　FUTURE

Future Perfect Continuous

future perfect continuous future

PAST　NOW　FUTURE

01 SIMPLE PRESENT 現在式

現在式又叫做簡單現在式，表面看起來很簡單，不就是表示現在嗎？不過，英文還有現在進行式 (Present Continuous Tense)，表示正在做的事，像 "我正在吃飯呢" 這樣的意思，就該用現在進行式，所以現在式另有用途。

1.1 怎樣用
Usage

用途

 A 永遠都真的現象

ALWAYS

 • The sun rises in the east.
• The earth travels round the sun.

甚麼是永恆現象呢？太陽從東方升起以及地球圍繞太陽轉當然是永恆現象。

用途

 B 經常會做的事

REPEATING

• Janice goes swimming every Saturday.
• Tim often visits his grandmother on Mondays.

怎麼知道是經常做的呢？這些例句裏就有表示頻率、表示重複做的副詞。這些副詞是指示詞 (signal words)，可以提醒你用現在式。

✚ **現在式的指示詞有：**

often, usually, always, every, sometimes, once a year, never.

✚ **比較中英文：**

如果我們把 "她正在上學" 說成 "She goes to school"，講英語的人可能把握不準你要講甚麼，你應該說："She is going to school"；如果要說她已到上學的年紀，你就要考慮別的表達方法了。

用途

 沒有特定時間、一直如此的狀態

STATE / FACT

 • Wendy is a teacher.
• The earth revolves around the sun.

表達一直都是這樣的 "狀態" (state)，並沒有特定開始或結束的時間。

1.2 文法運用格式速查表
Speed check

⭐ 現在式的構成形式

is/am/are + 動詞

➕ 1.2.1 表達肯定 Affirmative

主語	動詞 be	例子
第一身 I, we	am, are	I am glad to see you. We are friends.
第二身 you	are	You are welcome.
第三身 he, she, it	is	He is clever. She is a teacher. It is hot in the room.

✴ 1.2.2 動詞加 -s -es -ies 的規則

主語	動詞	加 -s -es -ies	例子
第一身 I, we	所有動詞	不加	eat
第二身 you	所有動詞	不加	eat
第三身 he, she, it	除了用 y 或 sh, ch, ss, x, zz, o 結尾的動詞	s	eat → eats
	元音字母 (a,e,i,o,u) + y	s	say → says preys → preys
	輔音字母 + y	ies	try → tries cry → cries

sh, ch, ss, x, zz, o 結尾	es	wash → wash<u>es</u> catch → catch<u>es</u> pass → pass<u>es</u> mix → mix<u>es</u> buzz → buzz<u>es</u> echo → echo<u>es</u>
第三身 they　所有動詞	不加	eat

➊ 1.2.3 表達否定 Negative

主語	don't, doesn't	例子
第一身 I, we	don't	I <u>don't</u> like playing football.
第二身 you	don't	You <u>don't</u> go to school on Sundays.
第三身 he, she, it	doesn't	She <u>doesn't</u> go hiking every Sunday.
第三身 they	don't	They <u>don't</u> like their Science teacher.

❓ 1.2.4 問問題 Asking Questions

第一種方法：動詞是 be

主語	be	提問	用否定語氣提問
第一身 I, we	am are	Am I right? Are we right?	Aren't / *Ain't I right? Aren't we right?
第二身 you	are	Are you sure?	Aren't you sure?
第三身 he, she, it	is	Is he right?	Isn't he right?
第三身 they	are	Are they right?	Aren't they right?

* ain't 是 am not 的口語說法

第二種方法：動詞不是 be *(is/am/are)*

主語	加	提問	用否定語氣提問
第一身 I, we 第二身 you	do	<u>Do</u> you know what I mean?	<u>Don't</u> you think I should buy this new camera?
第三身 he,she,it	does	<u>Does</u> James visit his grandmother on Sundays?	<u>Doesn't</u> she know that James has already moved to Los Angeles?
第三身 they	do	<u>Do</u> they plan to protest every Sunday?	<u>Don't</u> they understand my point?

❓ 1.2.5 附加疑問（Question tags）

想確認對方同意你的想法時用。注意，附加疑問常見於講話，少用於書寫。

am, is, are 及 aren't, isn't, aren't

am	I am not late, <u>am</u> I?
is	Tracy is not sick, <u>is</u> she?
are	You are not tired, <u>are</u> you?
ain't	I am late, <u>aren't</u> /<u>ain't</u> I?
isn't	Tracy is sick, <u>isn't</u> she?
aren't	You are tired, <u>aren't</u> you?

do, does 及 don't, doesn't

I have to pay for the camera bag, <u>don't</u> I?	I <u>do not</u> have to pay for the camera bag, <u>do</u> I?
You like swimming, <u>don't</u> you?	You <u>do not</u> like swimming, <u>do</u> you?
Tim often plays basketball, <u>doesn't</u> he?	Tim <u>does not</u> play basketball, <u>does</u> he?

02 PRESENT CONTINUOUS 現在進行式

現在的事用現在式,而現在這個時候或這段時間正在做的,就用現在
進行式。不過,現在進行式的用途比你想像中要多一點。

 ## 2.1 怎樣用
Usage

用途
 A **現在或近來這段時間的動作或狀態**

PAST NOW FUTURE

- What are you writing now?
- At this moment she is watching a movie.
- I am reading good book. It is about space adventure.

➕ **現在進行式的提示詞有:**

now, at present, at this moment, at this time, still, still now, any longer,
any more, even now.

用途
 B **兩個同時發生的動作,時間較長的用現在進行式**

- I am playing an on-line game when my dog suddenly jumps at me.
- Jane is listening to music when she is on her way to school.

當兩個動作現在發生,發生時間較長的用現在進行式,以表達背
景;發生時間較短的動作用現在式 (參見單元 1)。

when 和 while 是常見的提示詞。

用途

兩個同時發生的動作，時間一樣長，兩個都用
現在進行式

PAST　　　NOW　　　FUTURE

- My father is reading the newspaper while my brother is listening to music.
- Jimmy is sleeping while his wife is preparing his breakfast.

用途

表示現在習慣或經常性動作

PAST　　　NOW　　　FUTURE

- Wendy is always caring about his son.
- You are forever complaining.

注意，這種用法帶有感情色彩，如以上例句中，說話者對 Wendy 表示讚賞，對 you 表示討厭。若用現在式，那麼只是客觀敘述，不帶個人感受。

⊕ **比較中英文：**

別以為 always, forever 只可用現在式（參見單元 1），它可用於現在進行式來表示習慣。而這種用法的 always，比較像中文裏的 "總是"，像上面例句，"你總是投訴" 比 "你常常投訴" 語氣更貼切。

2.2 文法運用格式速查表
Speed check

⭐ 現在進行式的構成形成

is/am/are + 現在分詞

➕ 2.2.1 表達肯定 Affirmative

主語	動詞	例子
第一身 I	am + 現在分詞	I am doing homework now.
第一身 we	are + 現在分詞	We are having a meeting.
第二身 you	are + 現在分詞	You are drawing.
第三身 he, she, it	is + 現在分詞	He/She is listening to the radio. It is moving.
第三身 they	are + 現在分詞	They are playing in the football field.

➖ 2.2.2 表達否定 Negative

主語	am/is/are not doing	例子
第一身 I	am not (ain't) + 現在分詞	I am not doing homework now.
第一身 we	are not (aren't) + 現在分詞	We are not playing TV games.
第二身 you	are not (aren't) + 現在分詞	You aren't watching movie.

第三身 he, she, it	is not (isn't) + 現在分詞	He/She is not feeling very well now. It is not moving now.
第三身 they	are not (aren't) + 現在分詞	They aren't having a meeting at this moment.

❓ 2.2.3 問問題 Asking Questions

主語	動詞	提問	用否定語氣提問
第一身 I	am + 現在分詞	Am I doing this right?	Aren't I doing this right?
第一身 we	are + 現在分詞	Are we having a meeting at this moment?	Aren't we having a meeting at this moment?
第二身 you	are + 現在分詞	Are you listening to the radio?	Aren't you listening to the radio?
第三身 he, she, it	is + 現在分詞	Is he doing his homework right now?	Isn't he doing his homework right now?
第三身 they	are + 現在分詞	Are they having a meeting at this moment?	Aren't they having a meeting at this moment?

SIMPLE PAST 過去式

中文常用"過""剛才""以前""曾經"等表示過去發生的事,但英文就不是這麼簡單了。英文有時會用類似的提示詞,但有時不用,這時候就要從動詞的變化來理解是不是發生在過去了。

 ## 3.1 怎樣用
Usage

用途

A 過去發生的事或存在的狀態

PAST   NOW   FUTURE

例
- Who put forward the suggestion the other day?
- What was he ten years ago?
- I wasn't in last night.
- Where did you go just now?

怎麼知道是過去發生的動作呢?提示詞 (signal words),可以提醒你用過去式。

⊕ **過去式的提示詞有:**

just now, yesterday, last week, ago, the other day, in 2010.

用途

過去的習慣或經常性動作

- She often came to help us.
- Wherever the Browns went during their visit, they were given a warm welcome.
- We didn't have any money at that time.

用途

過去發生，但發生的時間不清楚

- I was glad to get your e-mail.
- What was the final score?
- How did you like the movie?
- I thought you were not in.
- It was a pity you didn't go with us.

用途

D 用 wish、wonder、think、hope 的過去式，詢問、請求或建議

- I thought you might have some.
- Everyone wished to meet us.

⊕ **比較：**

過去式表示的動作或狀態已成過去，已不存在。

Christine was an invalid all her life. ←→ Christine has been an invalid all her life.

（她已不在人世） ←→ （她還活着）

Mrs. Darby lived in Texas for seven years. ←→ Mrs. Darby has lived in Texas for seven years.

（她已不住在德克薩斯州） ←→ （她還住在德克薩斯州，有可能指剛搬走。）

注意，用過去式表示現在的時間，可表達委婉語氣。

例如用 want, hope, wonder, think, intend 等：

　　Did you want anything else?

　　I wondered if you could lend me your car.

例如情態動詞 could 和 would：

　　Could you lend me your bike?

3.2 文法運用格式速查表
Speed check

⭐ 過去式的構成形式

was/were + 動詞

➕ 3.2.1 表達肯定 Affirmative

主語	動詞 be	例子
第一身 I ,we	was, were	I was glad to join the magic show. We were classmates.
第二身 you	were	You were at the airport last night.
第三身 he, she, it	was	He was a policeman. She was a teacher. It was hot in the room.

⬛ 3.2.2 動詞加 -d -ed -ied 的規則

主語	動詞	加 -d -ed -ied	例子
第一身 I ,we 第二身 you 第三身 he, she, it 第三身 they	一般情況	ed	want → wanted
	不發音的 e	d	live → lived like → liked
	輔音字母 + y	y → ied	try → tried study → studied (但 stay → stayed，這是因為 y 前面是母音字母的動詞是規則動詞)
	重讀閉音節 *	重複最後的輔音字母後，加 -ed	plan → planned stop → stopped permit → permitted prefer → preferred (例外：opened, attacked)

* 閉音節以輔音 (consonant) 結尾。

❑ 3.2.3 不規則動詞（irregular verbs）

不用 -ed 構成過去式，要留心去記。很煩？不用怕，它們的變化也有一些原則。

不規則動詞的變化原則

	變化原則	例
1	i → a	begin → began drink → drank give → gave ring → rang sing → sang sit → sat swim → swam
2	重讀開音節中的 i → o （開音節：以元音結尾的音節，如 no）	drive → drove ride → rode write → wrote
3	aw / ow → ew	draw → drew grow → grew know → knew throw → threw （例外：show → showed，snow → snowed）
4	e → o	get → got forget → forgot
5	ee → e	feed → fed meet → met
6	eep → ept	keep → kept sleep → slept sweep → swept
7	eak → oke	break → broke speak → spoke
8	ell → old	sell → sold tell → told
9	an → oo	stand → stood understand → understood
10	以 ought 和 aught 結尾	bring → brought buy → bought think → thought catch → caught teach → taught

11	以 ould 結尾的情態動詞	can → could shall → should will → would
12	o → a	come → came become → became
13	動詞後加 d 或 t，且發生音變	hear → heard say → said mean → meant
14	形式不變	let → let must → must put → put read → read /red cut → cut
15	不符合上述規律的動詞過去式	am / is → was are → were build → built do → did eat → ate fall → fell feel → felt find → found fly → flew go → went have / has → had hold → held leave → left make → made may → might run → ran see → saw take → took sit → sat

＊注意，附錄有不規則動詞表。

➖ 3.2.4 表達否定 Negative

主語	was/were not, did not do	例子
第一身 I	was not (wasn't) did not (didn't) + 動詞原形	I wasn't sad. I did not work there.
第一身 we	were not (weren't) did not (didn't) + 動詞原形	We were not there. We didn't play badminton.
第二身 you	were not (weren't) did not (didn't) + 動詞原形	You didn't come to the party.
第三身 he, she, it	was not (wasn't) did not (didn't) + 動詞原形	He didn't buy the guitar.
第三身 they	were not (weren't) did not (didn't) + 動詞原形	They weren't university students.

❓ 3.2.5 問問題 Asking Questions

第一種方法：動詞是 be

主語	be	提問	用否定語氣提問
第一身 I	was	Was I right?	Wasn't I right?
第一身 we	were	Were we right?	Weren't we right?
第二身 you	were	Were you sure?	Weren't you sure?
第三身 he, she, it	was	Was he right?	Wasn't he right?
第三身 they	were	Were they right?	Weren't they right?

第二種方法：動詞不是 be (is / am / are)

主語	加	提問	用否定語氣提問
第一身 I, we	did	Did I answer the question correctly?	Didn't I answer the question correctly?
第二身 you	did	Did you know what I mean?	Didn't you know what I mean?
第三身 he, she, it	did	Did James visit his grandmother last Sunday?	Didn't James visit his grandmother last Sunday?
第三身 they	did	Did they understand my point?	Didn't they understand my point?

 ## 3.3 過去式的口訣

⊕ **學好過去式，以下規則要記清：**

肯定句的過去式，be 要改成 was 或 were。
規則動詞加 -ed，不規則要一一記。
否定形式疑問句，無 be 記住加 did。
如把 did 放在前，別忘動詞還原形。

 ## 3.4 句型

It is time for sb to do sth 表示 "到……時間" 或 "該（做）……了"，
但想表示 "時間已遲了或早該這樣"，則用 It is time sb did sth。比
較下面例句：
It is time for you to go to bed. ⟷ It is time you went to bed.
（你該睡覺了。）   ⟷ （你早該睡覺了。）
用 would (had) rather sb did sth 表示 "寧願某人做某事"，例如：
I'd rather you came tomorrow.

04 PAST CONTINUOUS 過去進行式

講過去某個時刻正在做的動作或者所處的狀態。

4.1 怎樣用
Usage

用途

A 過去一個時間點或一段時間進行的動作

PAST　　NOW　　FUTURE

例
- What were you doing at this time last night?
- At that time she was working in a nursery.
- We were having lunch when they arrived.
- During the summer of 1999 she was travelling in Europe.

➕ **過去進行式的提示詞有：**

this morning, yesterday morning/afternoon/evening, from nine to ten last evening.

用途

B 兩個同時在過去進行的動作，時間較長的用過去進行式表示背景

例
- I was reading the newspaper when the doorbell rang.
- I met Diana while I was shopping this morning.
- My brother fell and hurt himself while he was riding his bicycle.

在過去有兩個動作同時發生，時間較長的動作用過去進行式，表示談話背景；時間較短的用過去式（參見單元3）。

常見提示詞有：

when, while.

注意，在過去一種狀態或情況中，也可用過去進行式表示背景。

 ● It was a dark night and a strong wind was blowing.

用途

C 兩個同時在過去進行的動作，當所需時間相同，可用過去進行式

 ● Last night I was doing my homework while he was listening to music.

 比較中英文：

用中文表達在過去 "正在做某事" 時，做事的時間長短對中文動詞並無影響，但用英文表達時，指某事所需時間較短要用過去式（參見單元 3），指某事所需時間較長用過去進行式，若兩者所需時間一樣，則用過去進行式。

用途

D 過去的習慣及經常性動作

PAST　　NOW　　FUTURE

 ● Tom was always thinking of others.
● Jenny was forever coming late.

 常見提示詞有：

always, forever.

注意，類似用法已在 Present Continuous Tense（參見單元 2）出現過，唯一不同的是經常性動作在過去已經發生。

用途

表示過去的將來

 • He said he was leaving home in a day or two.
• I knew that the plane was taking off in a few minutes.

⊕ **常見提示詞有：**

go, come, leave, start, take off.

4.2 文法運用格式速查表
Speed check

★ 過去進行式的構成形式

was/were + 現在分詞

➕ 4.2.1 表達肯定 Affirmative

主語	動詞	例子
第一身 I	was + 現在分詞	I was working.
第一身 we	were + 現在分詞	We were playing.
第二身 you	were + 現在分詞	You were studying.
第三身 he, she, it	was + 現在分詞	He/She/It was eating.
第三身 they	were + 現在分詞	They were painting.

➖ 4.2.2 表達否定 Negative

主語	was/were not doing	例子
第一身 I	was not (wasn't) + 現在分詞	I wasn't feeling very well that day.
第一身 we	were not (weren't) + 現在分詞	We weren't doing projects this morning.
第二身 you	were not (weren't) + 現在分詞	You weren't doing revision yesterday.
第三身 he, she, it	was not (wasn't) + 現在分詞	He/She/It wasn't doing homework last night.
第三身 they	were not (weren't) + 現在分詞	They weren't having a meeting at that time

❓ 4.2.3 問問題 Asking Questions

主語	動詞	提問	用否定語氣提問
第一身 I	was + 現在分詞	Was I correct?	Wasn't I correct?
第一身 we	were + 現在分詞	Were we correct?	Weren't we correct?
第二身 you	were + 現在分詞	Were you doing homework this morning?	Weren't you doing homework this morning?
第三身 he, she, it	was + 現在分詞	Was he/she doing his/her homework at nine last night?	Wasn't he/she doing his/her homework at nine last night?
第三身 they	were + 現在分詞	Were they having a meeting at that time?	Weren't they having a meeting at that time?

05 PRESENT PERFECT 現在完成式

現在完成式 (Present Perfect Tense)，指在過去開始的動作已完成，但這動作對現在有影響。

5.1 怎樣用
Usage

➕ **比較：**

現在完成式和過去式（參見單元 3）同樣指動作在過去開始，但現在完成式指動作與現在仍有關係，過去式指動作對現在沒有影響。

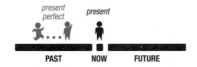

A 過去發生的事，影響現在的狀態

- She has passed the driving test at last.
- I have just tidied up the bedroom since I returned home.

➕ **現在完成式的指示詞有：**

just, at last, recently, finally, already.

➕ **比較中英文：**

中文沒有特別細分過去已發生的動作是否對現在仍有影響，很少理會這個動作是否影響現在。這與英文不同，英文會細分。

用途

B 已經經過一段時間，而現在已完成的動作

例
- He has worked here since 2010.
- I have painted half of the house so far this morning.

➕ **表示動作的持續性的提示詞有：**

for, up till now, since, up to the present, so far.

➕ **比較現在完成式和過去式（參見單元 3）：**

He has worked here since 2010. ⟷ He worked here.

過去式 "He worked here."，只是簡單點出 "他曾經在這裏工作" 這個事實，沒有強調他甚麼時候開始在這裏工作，以及持續工作多久。而 "He has worked here since 2010." 就指出他開始在這裏工作的時間，沒有表示他現在是否有繼續做。

如果你想表達他已經工作了四年，但現已沒有繼續做下去，你可以說成 "He has worked here for 4 years."。

5.2 文法運用格式速查表
Speed check

★ **現在完成式的構成形式**

have / has + 過去分詞

➕ **5.2.1 表達肯定 Affirmative**

主語	動詞	例子
第一身 I, we	have + 過去分詞	I have tidied up the room.
第二身 you	have + 過去分詞	You have passed the exam.
第三身 he, she, it	has + 過去分詞	He has worked here for 10 years.
第三身 they	have + 過去分詞	They have worked on the project.

➖ **5.2.2 表達否定 Negative**

主語	have not / never done	例子
第一身 I, we	have not (haven't) / have never + 過去分詞	I have not met Bonnie since last summer.
第二身 you	have not (haven't) / have never + 過去分詞	You haven't passed the driving test yet.
第三身 he, she, it	has not (hasn't) / has never + 過去分詞	Mary has never been to France.
第三身 they	have not (haven't) / have never + 過去分詞	They have never met the CEO.

❓ 5.2.3 問問題 Asking Questions

主語	動詞	提問	用否定語氣提問
第一身 I, we	have + (ever) + 過去分詞	Have we met Bonnie since she came back?	Haven't we met Bonnie since she came back?
第二身 you	have + (ever) + 過去分詞	Have you passed the driving test?	Haven't you passed the driving test?
第三身 he, she, it	has + (ever) + 過去分詞	Has Tom finished his project?	Hasn't Tom finished his project?
第三身 they	have + (ever) + 過去分詞	Have they ever played a real football match?	Haven't they ever played a real football match?

06 PRESENT PERFECT CONTINUOUS 現在完成進行式

現在完成進行式 (Present Perfect Continuous Tense) 表示動作在過去發生，直至現在仍未完成。

6.1 怎樣用
Usage

用途

 在過去發生，直至現在仍在繼續

PAST　　NOW　　FUTURE

例
- She has been studying for her final exam.
- John has been finding a way to help his son quit smoking.

➕ **現在完成進行式的提示詞有：**
recently, these days, since the last night, for a long time, for four weeks/three months/two years.

➕ **比較：**
現在完成進行式表示在過去發生但仍進行的動作，不同於表示動作已完成的現在完成式。

例
- She has been studying for her exam. ⟶ She has studied for her exam.
  （動作未完）　　　　　　　　　　　　　⟶ （動作已完）

- He has been trying to help his son. ⟶ He has tried to help his son.
  （動作未完）　　　　　　　　　　　　　⟶ （動作已完）

⚡ 6.2 文法運用格式速查表
Speed check

⭐ 現在完成進行式的構成形式

has / have been + 現在分詞

➕ 6.2.1 表達肯定 Affirmative

主語	動詞	例子
第一身 I, we	have been + 現在分詞	I have been doing well. We have been doing well.
第二身 you	have been + 現在分詞	You have been working.
第三身 he, she, it	has been + 現在分詞	He has been thinking.
第三身 they	have been + 現在分詞	They have been working.

➖ 6.2.2 表達否定 Negative

主語	have / has not been doing	例子
第一身 I, we	have not (haven't) been + 現在分詞	I have not been visiting Bonnie recently.
第二身 you	have not (haven't) been + 現在分詞	You haven't been hanging out with Tom for a month.
第三身 he, she, it	has not (hasn't) been + 現在分詞	Jenny has not been working on the project.
第三身 they	have not (haven't) been + 現在分詞	They have not been working on the project.

❓ 6.2.3 問問題 Asking Questions

主語	動詞	提問	用否定語氣提問
第一身 I, we	have been + 現在分詞	Have we been making the situation worse?	Haven't we been making the situation worse?
第二身 you	have been + 現在分詞	Have you been playing tennis these days?	Haven't you been playing tennis these days?
第三身 he, she, it	has been + 現在分詞	Has Tom been studying for his exam?	Hasn't Tom been studying for his exam?
第三身 they	have been + 現在分詞	Have they been working on the project?	Haven't they been working on the project?

07 PAST PERFECT 過去完成式

我們已知道過去式（參見單元 3）可表示已發生的事，但如果一件事發生在過去的過去，那可以怎樣表示呢？這時就要用到過去完成式了。

7.1 怎樣用
Usage

用途

A 表示 "過去的過去" 已發生的事

past perfect *past*

PAST   NOW   FUTURE

- He had left when I arrived.
- She had not finished her breakfast when the phone rang.
- By the time the police came the robbers had not left.

"表示過去的過去" 是指一個動作在過去某個時間之前已經完成。

➕ **常見提示詞有：**

when, by, before.

用途

表示過去某時間之前發生的動作，到某時間結束或繼續

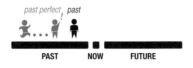

past perfect | past

PAST　　NOW　　FUTURE

- When Jack arrived, he learned Mary had been away for almost an hour.
- He had stayed here for two days before he left.
- He said he had worked in that factory since 1949.

⊕ **常見的提示動詞有：**

told, said, knew, heard, thought 等，在這些動詞之後用過去完成式。
此外，還用於表示意向的動詞如 hope, wish, expect, think, intend,
mean, suppose 等，以表示遺憾或後悔。

- We had hoped that you would come, but you didn't.
- They had expected to be able to arrive before ten.
- They had wanted to help but could not get there in time.

⚡ 7.2 文法運用格式速查表
Speed check

✪ 過去完成式的構成形式

had + 過去分詞

➕ 7.2.1 表達肯定 Affirmative

主語	動詞	例子
第一身 I, we	had + 過去分詞	I/We had finished the work when they arrived.
第二身 you	had + 過去分詞	You had finished the work when they arrived.
第三身 he, she, it	had + 過去分詞	He/She/It had finished the work when they arrived.
第三身 they	had + 過去分詞	They had finished the work when we arrived.

➖ 7.2.2 表達否定 Negative

主語	had not done	例子
第一身 I, we	had not + 過去分詞	I/We had not yet finished the work when they arrived.
第二身 you	had not + 過去分詞	You had not yet finished the work when they arrived.
第三身 he, she, it	had not + 過去分詞	He/She/It had not yet finished the work when they arrived.
第三身 they	had not + 過去分詞	They had not yet finished the work when we arrived.

❓ 7.2.3 問問題 Asking Questions

主語	動詞	提問	用否定語氣提問
第一身 I, we	had + 過去分詞	Had I/we planned the rundown of the trip?	Hadn't I/we planned the rundown of the trip?
第二身 you	had + 過去分詞	Had you learned some Chinese before you came to China?	Hadn't you learned some Chinese before you came to China?
第三身 he, she, it	had + 過去分詞	Had he/she/it learned some Chinese before he/she/it came to China?	Hadn't he/she/it learned some Chinese before he/she/it came to China?
第三身 they	had + 過去分詞	Had they learned some Chinese before they came to China?	Hadn't they learned some Chinese before you they came to China?

7.3 句型

7.3.1 用於 hardly…when…; no sooner…than…; It was the first (second, etc) time (that)…等

• Hardly had he begun to speak when the audience interrupted him.
• No sooner had he arrived than he went away again.
• It was the third time that he had been out of work that year.

留意到例句的結構嗎？請記住，表示強調時，要將 "hardly ... when ... ; no sooner ... than ..." 放在句首，並一定要用倒裝語序。

比較：

過去完成式強調 "過去的過去"，而過去式強調相對於現在的過去，兩者用不同的時間狀語。

They had arrived by ten yesterday. (強調昨天 10 點之前已經到達。)
They arrived at ten yesterday. (強調在昨天 10 點到達。)

如果沒有時間狀語如 by ten yesterday 或 at ten yesterday ，那就要按上下文判斷動作發生的先後：先發生的用過去完成式，後發生的用過去式。

• She was very happy. Her whole family was pleased with her, too. She had just won the first in the composition competition.
• Mr. Smith died yesterday. He had been a good friend of mine.
• I didn't know a thing about the verbs, for I had not studied my lesson.

當兩個或兩個以上接連發生的動作用 and 或 but 連接時，如按時間順序寫出，只需用過去式；假如句子內有 before、after、as soon as 等表，可用過去式代替過去完成式。

• He entered the room, turned on the light and watched the TV.
• I lost my pen but soon found it.
• After he arrived in England, Marx worked hard to improve his English.
• Many people left for home before the film ended.

08 PAST PERFECT CONTINUOUS 過去完成進行式

過去、完成、進行並存的時態聽上去很複雜，是不是？下圖可以幫你明白它的原理。

 8.1 怎樣用
Usage

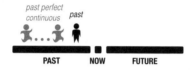

例 | • He had been watching TV before his father returned home.
爸爸已回家，所以用 returned，爸爸回家之前他已開始看電視，並且仍在看，所以用過去完成進行式。

⊕ **比較：**
過去完成進行式，指動作到過去某一個時間還未完，而過去完成式，指動作在過去某一個時間已完成。

用途

 強調動作仍在進行

例 | • He had been writing the novel.
| • Up to that time he had been translating those books.
動作在過去某個時間之前開始，延續到過去某個時間，但沒有表示是否已完結。

用途

B 表示重複或不斷發生

- He had been studying the meaning of this proverb.
- I had been studying the meaning of the poem.
- He had been quarrelling with his wife.

用途

C 表示突然，與 when 從句連用

- I had only been reading a few minutes when he came in.
- I had been sleeping when my friend telephone me.

8.2 文法運用格式速查表
Speed check

★ 過去完成進行式的構成形式

had been + 現在分詞

➕ 8.2.1 表達肯定 Affirmative

主語	動詞	例子
第一身 I, we	had been + 現在分詞	I / We had been working all the time.
第二身 you	had been + 現在分詞	You had been working all the time.
第三身 he, she, it	had been + 現在分詞	He/She/It had been working all the time.
第三身 they	had been + 現在分詞	They had been working all the time.

➖ 8.2.2 表達否定 Negative

主語	had not been doing	例子
第一身 I, we	had not been + 現在分詞	I / We had not been waiting for you.
第二身 you	had not been + 現在分詞	You had not been waiting for us.
第三身 he, she, it	had not been + 現在分詞	He/She/It had not been waiting for you.
第三身 they	had not been + 現在分詞	They had not been waiting for you.

過去完成進行式很少用於否定句，多用過去完成式取代。如果想表達 "他那時已多年不練習英語"，往往會說：

He had not practised English for many years.

而很少會說：

He had not been practicing English for many years.

但是，很少並不等於沒有。看看以下這個例外情況：

Rafael was scolded even though he hadn't been doing anything wrong.

❓ 8.2.3 問問題 Asking Questions

主語	動詞	提問	用否定語氣提問
第一身 I, we	had been + 現在分詞	Had I/we been expecting the news for some time?	Hadn't I/we been expecting the news for some time?
第二身 you	had been + 現在分詞	Had you been expecting the news for some time?	Hadn't you been expecting the news for some time?
第三身 he, she, it	had been + 現在分詞	Had he/she/it been expecting the news for some time?	Hadn't he/she/it been expecting the news for some time?
第三身 they	had been + 現在分詞	Had they been expecting the news for some time?	Hadn't they been expecting the news for some time?

09 SIMPLE FUTURE 將來式

將來式 (Simple Future) 表示將來某個時間發生的動作、事情或狀態。

9.1 怎樣用
Usage

PAST　　NOW　　FUTURE

例如，想表達 "我明天要去游泳" 或 "她明年會上大學"，就要用將來式。但將來式的用途可止一個。

用途

A 將來某個時刻的動作或狀態

- We will have a meeting tomorrow.
- The agreement will come into force next spring.
- We shall/will come to see you the day after tomorrow.

⊕ 將來式常見的提示詞有：

tomorrow, soon, next week, later, from now on, in the future.

用途

B 將來某段時間經常發生的動作或狀態

- We shall come and work in this factory every year.
- The students will come and work in the lab once a week.
- He will soon become a university student.

以上例句都含有提示詞，但如果沒有提示詞，你就要靠上下文來決定那是否指未來發生的動作或狀態。

- I think he will tell us the truth.
- Who'll take the chair?
- The meeting won't last long.

用途 C 表示純屬客觀的將來

- You will be forty years old next year.
- Tomorrow will be Sunday again.

用途 D 表示說話者的決定或意圖

- I feel ill now, and I'll go to see the doctor.
- Joe: Can somebody help me?
  Esther: I will.

用途 E 表示一種習慣或傾向

PAST　　NOW　　FUTURE

- A drowning man will catch at a straw.
- Whoever fails to see this will make a big mistake.
- Susan will be happy with the good result.

用途 E 的否定式表示 "不能"、"沒法"，不要理解成將來才不能啊。

45

- The result is dissatisfied. Susan won't be happy with that. （蘇珊無法感到高興。）
- The machine won't work. （這機器壞了。）
- The play won't act. （這劇本無法上演。）

用途

 表示預測、揣測

- The man in the middle will be the visiting minister.
- I think it will rain this evening.

9.2 文法運用格式速查表
Speed check

★ 將來式的構成形式

shall / will + 動詞原形

➕ 9.2.1 表達肯定 Affirmative

主語	動詞	例子
第一身 I, we	shall / will ('ll) + 動詞原形	We shall finish all the work by noon.
第二身 you	will ('ll) + 動詞原形	You'll meet Jacky at the station this evening.
第三身 he, she, it	will ('ll) + 動詞原形	Mary will buy a new piano tomorrow.
第三身 they	will ('ll) + 動詞原形	They'll have a match in the coming Friday.

* 注意，當主語為第一身時，一般用 shall，但它常被 will 代替。（如 shall 用於陳述句的第二、三人稱，它表示的不是時態，而成了情態動詞，意思為 "應該"、"必須"。）

✦ 9.2.2 表達否定 Negative

主語	shall not / will not do	例子
第一身 I, we	shall not (shan't) / will not (won't) + 動詞原形	I shan't leave the work until tomorrow.
第二身 you	will not (won't) + 動詞原形	You will not finish the job today.
第三身 he, she, it	will not (won't) + 動詞原形	He won't go to the concert.
第三身 they	will not (won't) + 動詞原形	They will not attend the meeting.

❓ 9.2.3 問問題 Asking Questions

主語	動詞	提問	用否定語氣提問
第一身 I, we	shall/will ('ll) + 動詞原形	Shall I close the door? Shall we go there?	Shan't I close the door? Shan't we go there?
第二身 you	will ('ll) + 動詞原形	Will you be at home this evening?	Won't you be at home this evening?
第三身 he, she, it	will ('ll) + 動詞原形	Will she be a musician?	Won't she be a musician?
第三身 they	will ('ll) + 動詞原形	Will they go to the show?	Won't they go to the show?

* 注意，will 在陳述句可用於各個人稱，但在徵求意見，或就說話人向對方提請求時，多用疑問句，並多用第二身。如：

Will you pass me that cup?

Will you (please) help me with maths?

Will you please lend me your pen?

9.3 句型

用 if 開頭的條件句，一般不用將來式，而是用現在式

- What shall we do if he doesn't come?
- If it doesn't rain tomorrow, we will go out for a picnic.

只有以下兩種情況 if- 條件句才可用將來式。

(1) 表示願望：

If they won't cooperate, our plan will fall flat（落空）.

(2) 主句謂語表示現在情況：

If he won't arrive this morning, why should we wait here?

10 FUTURE CONTINUOUS 將來進行式

主要表示將來某個時間正在做的動作，或開始做下去的動作。

10.1 怎樣用
Usage

PAST   NOW   FUTURE

用途

A 將來某個時間正在做的動作

 例
- He will be working at this time next Monday
- When he comes to my house tomorrow, I will be writing the report.
- By this time tomorrow, I'll be lying on the beach.

➕ **將來進行式的提示詞有：**

tomorrow, soon, this evening, in two days, on Sunday, tomorrow evening, by this time.

用途

B 預測將來會做

例
- Tomorrow I will be flying to Beijing.
- We'll be having a meeting at three o'clock tomorrow afternoon.
- After you take the medicine, you will be feeling much better.

表示委婉客氣

• When shall we be meeting again?
• When will you be putting on another performance?

注意，以上例句也可用將來式（參見單元 9），但會使語氣顯得生硬，有點太直接。用將來進行式較自然及合乎外國人習慣。

⚡ 10.2 文法運用格式速查表
Speed check

⭐ 將來進行式的構成形式

shall / will + be + 現在分詞

➕ 10.2.1 表達肯定 Affirmative

主語	動詞	例子
第一身 I, we	shall / will + be + 現在分詞	I shall / will be leaving. We shall/will be playing.
第二身 you	will + be + 現在分詞	You will be studying.
第三身 he, she, it	will + be + 現在分詞	He/She/It will be leaving.
第三身 they	will + be + 現在分詞	They will be coming.

➖ 10.2.2 表達否定 Negative

主語	shall not / will not be doing	例子
第一身 I, we	shall not (shan't) / will not (won't) + be + 現在分詞	I shall / will not be working. We shall / will not be playing.
第二身 you	will not (won't) + be + 現在分詞	You will not be studying.
第三身 he, she, it	will not (won't) + be + 現在分詞	He/She/It will not be leaving.
第三身 they	will not (won't) + be + 現在分詞	They will not be coming.

❓ 10.2.3 問問題 Asking Questions

主語	動詞	提問	用否定語氣提問
第一身 I, we	shall / will + be + 現在分詞	Shall / Will I be working? Shall / Will we be playing?	Shan't / Won't I be working? Shan't / Won't we be playing?
第二身 you	will + be + 現在分詞	Will you be studying?	Won't you be studying?
第三身 he, she, it	will + be + 現在分詞	Will he / She / It be leaving?	Won't he / she / it be leaving?
第三身 they	will + be + 現在分詞	Will they be coming?	Won't they be coming?

11 FUTURE PERFECT 將來完成式

將來的事又怎麼會完成呢？其實它是表示到將來某個時間為止必會完成或預計要完成的動作。

11.1 怎樣用
Usage

用途

A 表示動作在將來某個時間之前完成

 • We shall have finished the project by the end of this term.
• By the time you get home I will have cleaned the house from top to bottom.
• By the year 2030 scientists will probably have discovered a cure for cancer.

➕ **將來完成式的常見的提示詞有：**
before 和 by the time.
注意，完成的動作會對將來產生影響。

用途

表示一直進行到將來某個時間為止的狀態

 ・ We shall have been married for 20 years by then.
・ By the end of next month he will have been here for ten years.
・ By the mid-21st century China will have become very prosperous.

用途

猜測

 ・ We worked together for a year. He won't have forgotten me.
・ They will have arrived home by now.
・ You will have heard this. I guess.
・ Will you have known him for ten years next month?
注意，有時可用現在完成式（參見單元 5）代替將來完成式，來表示將來某個時間已完成的動作。如：

You'll get to like the subject after you have studied it for some time.

I'll go to see the exhibition as soon as I've finished my work.

11.2 文法運用格式速查表
Speed check

★ 將來完成式的構成形式

shall / will have + 過去分詞

➕ 11.2.1 表達肯定 Affirmative

主語	動詞	例子
第一身 I, we	shall / will + have + 過去分詞	I / We shall / will have finished all the work by the time you are back this evening.
第二身 you	will + have + 過去分詞	You will have finished all the work by the time we are back this evening.
第三身 he, she, it	will + have + 過去分詞	He / She / It will have finished all the work by the time you are back this evening.
第三身 they	will + have + 過去分詞	They will have finished all the work by the time you are back this evening.

➖ 11.2.2 表達否定 Negative

主語	shall not / will not have done	例子
第一身 I, we	shall not (shan't) / will not (won't) + have + 過去分詞	I / We shall / will have learned 12 units by the end of this term.
第二身 you	will not (won't) + have + 過去分詞	You will not have learned 12 units by the end of this term.
第三身 he, she, it	will not (won't) + have + 過去分詞	He / She / It will not have learned 12 units by the end of this term.
第三身 they	will not (won't) + have + 過去分詞	They will not have learned 12 units by the end of this term.

❓ 11.2.3 問問題 Asking Questions

主語	動詞	提問	用否定語氣提問
第一身 I, we	shall / will + have + 過去分詞	Shall / Will I / we have known Kevin for 10 years by next month?	Shan't / Won't I / we have known Kevin for 10 years by next month?
第二身 you	will + have + 過去分詞	Will you have known Kevin for 10 years by next month?	Won't you have known Kevin for 10 years by next month?
第三身 he, she, it	will + have + 過去分詞	Will he / she / it have known Kevin for 10 years by next month?	Won't he / she / it have known Kevin for 10 years by next month?
第三身 they	will + have + 過去分詞	Will they have known Kevin for 10 years by next month?	Won't they have known Kevin for 10 years by next month?

12 FUTURE PERFECT CONTINUOUS 將來完成進行式

將來完成的事怎麼會有進行式呢?它是表示動作從某個時間開始,一直延續到將來另一個時間為止。

12.1 怎樣用
Usage

➕ 常用提示詞是:by。

用途

 強調持續或經常

- By the end of May he will have been living here for ten years. (在未來十年將一直住在這裏)
- I shall have been working here for twenty years by the end of the year. (在年底之前將一直工作)

用途

 預測,猜測

- If we don't hurry up, the store will have been closing before we get there. (預測客觀事物)
- You'll have been wondering all this time how my invention works. (猜測別人的主觀意圖,will 有 "大概" 或 "我想" 的意思)

⊕ 比較：

將來完成式（參見單元 11）可表示動作持續，也可表示動作已完成。
但將來完成進行式只能表示持續的動作。

By the end of this year they will have learned English for ten years.（有可能繼續）

By the end of this term he will have been studying in this university for 5 years.（暗示動作會繼續）

注意，有些表示狀態的動詞如 have，不能用於將來完成進行式，只可以用於將來完成式（參見單元 11）。

⚡ 12.2 文法運用格式速查表
Speed check

✱ 將來完成進行式的構成形式

shall / will have been + 現在分詞

➕ 12.2.1 表達肯定 Affirmative

主語	動詞	例子
第一身 I, we	shall/will + have been + 現在分詞	I / We shall / will have been studying in this university for 4 years by the end of this semester.
第二身 you	will + have been + 現在分詞	You will have been studying in this university for 4 years by the end of this semester.
第三身 he, she, it	will + have been + 現在分詞	He / She / It will have been studying in this university for 4 years by the end of this semester.
第三身 they	will + have been + 現在分詞	They will have been studying in this university for 4 years by the end of this semester.

➖ 12.2.2 表達否定 Negative

主語	shall not / will not have been doing	例子
第一身 I, we	shall not (shan't) / will not (won't) + have been + 現在分詞	I / We shall / will not have been living here for 10 years by the end of this summer.
第二身 you	will not (won't) + have been + 現在分詞	You will not have been living here for 10 years by the end of this summer.

| 第三身 he, she, it | will not (won't) + have been + 現在分詞 | He / She / It will not have been living here for 10 years by the end of this summer. |
| 第三身 they | will not (won't) + have been + 現在分詞 | They will not have been living here for 10 years by the end of this summer. |

❓ 12.2.3 問問題 Asking Questions

主語	動詞	提問	用否定語氣提問
第一身 I, we	shall /will + have been + 現在分詞	Shall/Will I / we have been living here for 10 years by the end of this summer?	Shan't / Won't I / we have been living here for 10 years by the end of this summer?
第二身 you	will + have been + 現在分詞	Will you have been living here for 10 years by the end of this summer?	Won't you have been living here for 10 years by the end of this summer?
第三身 he, she, it	will + have been + 現在分詞	Will he / she / it have been living here for 10 years by the end of this summer?	Won't he / she / it have been living here for 10 years by the end of this summer?
第三身 they	will + have been + 現在分詞	Will they have been living here for 10 years by the end of this summer?	Won't they have been living here for 10 years by the end of this summer?

一個句子裏用現在式、過去式、未來式最好一致

綜合句子練習
Integrated Sentence Exercises

I 填空題

1 While we _____ (wait) for the bus, a girl _____ (run) up to us.

2 My grandmother _____ (be) dead.

3 Paul _____ (go) out with Jane after he _____ (make) a phone call.

4 When the chairman _____ (finish) speaking, he _____ (leave) the hall.

5 The Reads _____ (have) lunch when I _____ (get) to their house.

6 The crazy fans _____ (wait) patiently for two hours, and they would wait till the movie star arrived.

7 Peter: Was the driving pleasant when you had holidays in Guilin last summer?

Sally : No, it _____ (rain) for four days when we arrived, so the roads were very muddy.

8 The moment I got home, I found I _____ (leave) my jacket on the playground.

9 He said he _____ already _____ (give) the book to the teacher.

10 What do you think you _____ (do) at this time next year?

11 I suppose by the time I come back in ten years' time they _____ (pull down) all these old houses.

12 She _____ (not go) to Qingdao because she _____ (be) there before.

13 We _____ (paint) the house before we _____ (move) in.

14 _____ (do) you like playing football?

15 Sam _____ (travel) abroad twice a year.

16 I _____ (call) a friend when Bob _____ (come) in.

17 That rich old man _____ (make) a will before he _____ (die).

18 She fell ill because she _____ (work) too hard.

19 Jenny _____ (see) a big rainbow yesterday. A rainbow _____ (occur) when raindrops and sunshine _____ (cross) paths.

20 As soon as it _____ (stop) raining, they _____ (begin) working again.

21 It _____ (be) hot yesterday and most children _____ (play) outside.

22 By the time you arrive in London, we _____ (stay) in Europe for two weeks.

23 By the end of this year I _____ (save) enough money for a holiday.

24 What time _____ you _____ (get) to Beijing yesterday?

25 I _____ (study) here for four years by next summer.

26 Our plan _____ (fail) because we _____ (make) a bad mistake.

27 Tom _____ (say) he _____ (read) the book twice.

28 I _____ (turn off) all the lights before I _____ (go) to bed last night.

29 There _____ (be) a dolphin show in the zoo tomorrow evening.

30 I am sure he _____ (settle) the difficulties before you arrive.

31 We _____ (test) the new machine when the electricity _____ (go) off.

32 I _____ (be) to Shanghai before.

33 There _____ (be) enough milk at home last week, wasn't there?

34 What _____ (make) him cry just now?

35 Yesterday the teacher _____ (tell) us that the earth _____ (move) around the sun.

36 While mother _____ (put) Cathy to bed, the door bell _____ (ring).

37 Jim _____ (jump) on the bus as it _____ (move) away.

38 _____ your father _____ (go) to work every day last week?

39 It was quite late at night. George _____ (read) and Amy _____ (ply) her needle when they _____ (hear) a knock at the door.

40 She told me she _____ (be) to Sanya three times.

41 There _____ (be) not enough people to pick apples that day.

42 Mary _____ (read) a book when her brother _____ (play) an on-line game.

43 We _____ (get) to Beijing at 9:00 tomorrow evening.

44 They _____ (study) the map of the country before they _____ (leave).

45 The robbers _____ (run away) before the policemen _____ (arrive).

46 I hope that they _____ (repair) the road by the time we come back.

47 What are you doing, Jack? Making a model plane . I _____ (show) it in the science class at 10 o'clock tomorrow morning.

48 I'm afraid I won't be available. I _____ (see) a friend off at 2 o'clock this afternoon.

49 We were surprised at what she _____ already _____ (do).

50 There _____ (be) a serious traffic jam this morning and so Venice _____ (go) to school by Mass Transit Railway.

51 There _____ (be) a group round the fire when they _____ (reach) it. An old woman _____ (sit) on the ground near the kettle;

two small children _____ (lie) near her; a donkey _____ (bend) his head over a tall girl.

52 Were you surprised by the ending of the film? No. I _____ (read) the book.

53 She _____ (not want) to stay in bed while the others _____ (work) in the fields.

54 Even when she _____ (be) a child she _____ (think) of becoming a ballerina（芭蕾舞演員）.

55 I waited until he _____ (finish) his homework.

56 As I _____ (walk) in the park, it _____ (begin) to rain.

57 We _____ (learn) 4,000 English words by the end of this term.

58 Frank _____ (finish) his final year project before his graduation by the end of this semester.

59 Before I _____ (arrive) at the station, he _____ (leave).

60 He _____ (not tell) you the news of his wife's death.

61 By next July, Tom ___(1)___ (live) in our town for eight years and by the end of this year he ___(2)___ (teach) in the high school of our town for five years. He has never been away for long since he came here. But in a few days he ___(3)___ (leave) for Mediterranean Sea for a long holiday. Perhaps by this time next week he ___(4)___ (take) a sunbath on the beach. He ___(5)___ (enjoy) the sun and the delicious seafood there until the end of his holiday. During his absence some workers ___(6)___ (come) to repair his house. And the workers ___(7)___ (work) for his house for the whole 10 days. By the time when Tom comes back, they ___(8)___ (finish) their job.

II 畫以下句子的正確 timeline

1 Tommy often goes hiking on public holidays.

2 Judy is a nurse.

3 Flora is listening to music while her mother is cooking in the kitchen.

4 Cathy has worked in the Global Trading Company for four years.

5 Teresa visited Thailand last summer.

6 Wendy was having lunch with her friends when her mobile phone rang.

7 We have been living in London for over ten years.

8 John's father had died before John returned home.

9 Matthew had been finding ways to quit smoking before his grandfather, who had been smoking for thirty years, died of lung cancer.

10 They will be moving to New York when their daughter returns from Macau.

11 Peter will have been working for the Global Trading Company for ten years by the end of this year.

12 James will have completed the final term project before his graduation.

III 選擇題

1 The boy was delighted with his new story book which he _____ for a long time.
   A. was wanting
   B. has wanted
   C. has been wanting
   D. had been wanting

2 He is somebody now. He _____ his old classmates.
   A. will not remember
   B. will not have remembered
   C. does not remember
   D. has not remembered

3 By the end of this year, I _____ enough money for a holiday.
   A. will save
   B. will be saving
   C. will have saved
   D. have saved

4 It was midnight and he was tired because he _____ since dawn.
   A. was working
   B. has worked
   C. had been working
   D. has been working

5 I have been studying here for four years and by next summer I _____.
   A. shall graduate
   B. shall be graduated
   C. shall be graduating
   D. shall have graduated

6 When we get there, they _____ .
   A. will probably leave
   B. have probably left
   C. will probably have left
   D. probably left

7 He _____ to get her on the phone, but he didn't get through.
   A. has tried
   B. was trying

C. tries   D. had been trying

8 I hope her health _____ greatly by the time we come back next
   year.
   A. improves   B. improved
   C. will be improved   D. will have improved

9 I hope you _____ the instruction ready before I come tomorrow.
   A. to get   B. gets
   C. will get   D. will have gotten

10 By next summer I _____ here for 5 years.
   A. will work   B. shall have worked
   C. have worked   D. am working

11 Are you going to Richard's birthday party?
   Yes. By then I _____ my homework.
   A. had finished   B. will have finished
   C. would have finished   D. finished

12 He _____ the door and after that he had a drink at a small
   coffee shop.
   A. was painting   B. has painted
   C. had been painting   D. has been painting

13 His brother was good at playing table tennis. He _____ it since
   he was ten.
   A. had played   B. played
   C. had been playing   D. was playing

14 The man _____ there in the sun for a long time and got his face
    burnt.
    A. has stood   B. was standing
    C. had been standing   D. is standing

15 He said that he _____ the novel and had not finished it yet.
    A. is writing   B. has written
    C. writes   D. had been writing

16 I asked where they _____ all these days.
    A. have stayed   B. stay
    C. had been staying   D. were staying

17 She _____ from a bad cold when she took the exam.
    A. has suffered   B. had been suffering
    C. suffered   D. has been suffering

18 I suppose by the time I come back in ten years' time all these old
    house _____ down.
    A. will have been pulled   B. will be pulling
    C. will have pulled   D. will be pulled

19 I hope that they _____ the road by the time we come back.
    A. will have repaired   B. would have repaired
    C. have repaired   D. had repaired

20 They _____ for the bus a few moments when it came.
    A. had only been waiting   B. have only waited
    C. only waited   D. were only waiting

IV 翻譯以下句子

1 我們剛剛吃完早飯，他就進來了。

2 到下週三我就能將這本小說看完了。

3 他進來的時候，我已經努力修理電視機好幾個小時了。

4 等媽媽到家的時候，我看小寶寶早就睡熟了。

5 當時道路很危險。雨一直下了整整兩天。

6 不等我們趕到機場，飛機就會起飛的。

7 那男孩得到一輛新自行車很高興。他希望有一輛已經很久了。

8 明天這個時候她就在巴黎了。

9 當我們到達山頂時，太陽已經升起來了。

10 明年我父母就結婚 31 年了。

V 句型轉換

1 I sold the ticket when she arrived. (使本句變成否定句)

2 She had sung a song to us before she danced. (改用 did not sing，使本句變成否定句)

3 They began to climb the mountain after they had bought all the food. (改用 did not begin，使本句成為否定句)

4 By 10:00 a.m. John will have been very hungry. (改成疑問句)

5 Lucy had already completed the project when Mike arrived. (改成疑問句)

6　By the time he got to the airport, the plane had taken off. (改成疑問句)

7　He had broken his arm when I saw him. (用 what 開頭，改成疑問句)

8　When he had read the note, he went to the meeting place. (用 where 開頭，改成疑問句)

9　Jack didn't go to the cinema because he had seen the film. (用 why 開頭，改成疑問句)

10　We had had the toys for ten years before we gave them away.
　　(用 how long 開頭，改成疑問句)

11　She had written the book by the end of 1960. (用 what 開頭，改成疑問句)

12　We cooked the dumplings. We ate them up. (用過去完成式連接兩句)

13　Jim's father repaired the car. It was broken. (用過去完成式連接兩句)

14　We sat for our exams. Then we had a long holiday. (用過去完成式連接兩句) After we _____ , we _____.

15　He showed us a picture. Then he showed us around the house. (用過去完成式連接兩句) Before he _____ , he _____.

綜合篇章練習
Integrated Contextual Exercises

I

An interview

Host: Senator Smith, (1) _____ (thank) you for joining us.

Senator: Thank you so much for having me.

Host: The financial assets (2) _____ (shrink). Gasoline is above $3 a gallon. Tell us how your economic plan (3) _____ (take) us higher.

Senator: Well, (4) _____ (start with) dealing with the immediate crisis, both in the financial markets and in the housing market. And obviously, those things (5) _____ (connect).

On the housing market, I (6) _____ (think) it is important for us to create some bottom, giving people some sense of where this (7) _____ (end). The government should (8) _____ (step) in to help stabilize the market. It's not a bailout for borrowers or lenders, but what it (9) _____ (say) is we (10) _____ (rework) some of these loan packages so that they're affordable. And, you know, everybody's going to have to take a haircut, the borrowers and the lenders, but it won't be as bad as if a foreclosure took place.

Step number two, I think we (11) _____ (stabilize) and (12) _____ (provide) confidence in the financial markets. It is important to make sure that we (13) _____ (couple) that with some new regulatory structures.

The third thing is to understand that the economy has been out of balance for quite some time. We (14) _____ (have) high corporate profits, enormous rises in productivity over the last decade but wages and incomes (15) _____ (flat-line). And so you (16) _____ (have) a lot of concentrated wealth at the top, but ordinary folks (17) _____ (hammer) with rising gas prices, rising costs of health care, rising costs of college tuition.

And so creating a tax code that is more equitable and making sure that we (18) _____ (make) investments in things like infrastructure and clean energy can put us on a more stable long-term competitive footing. I think that has to be part of the package as well.

II

You and the atomic bomb by George Orwell

We were once told that the aeroplane (1) _____ (abolish) frontiers; actually it is only since the aeroplane became a serious weapon that frontiers (2)_____ (become) definitely impassable. The radio was once expected to promote international understanding and co-operation; it (3)_____ (turn) out to be a means of insulating one nation from another. The atomic bomb may complete the process by robbing the exploited classes and peoples of all power to revolt, and at the same time putting the possessors of the bomb on a basis of military equality. Unable to conquer one another, they are likely to continue ruling the world between them, and it is difficult to see how the balance can be upset except by slow and unpredictable demographic changes.

For forty or fifty years past, Mr. H.G. Wells and others (4) _____ (warn) us that man is in danger of destroying himself with his own weapons, leaving the ants or some other gregarious species to take over. Anyone who (5) _____ (see) the ruined cities of Germany (6) _____ (find)

this notion at least thinkable. Nevertheless, looking at the world as a whole, the drift for many decades (7) _____ (be) not towards anarchy but towards the reimposition of slavery. We may (8) _____ (head) not for general breakdown but for an epoch as horribly stable as the slave empires of antiquity. James Burnham's theory (9) _____ much _____ (discuss), but few people (10) _____ yet _____ (consider) its ideological implications – that is, the kind of world-view, the kind of beliefs, and the social structure that (11) _____ probably_____ (prevail) in a state which was at once unconquerable and in a permanent state of "cold war" with its neighbors.

III

Of human bondage by W. Somerset Maugham

The day (1)_____ (break) gray and dull. The clouds (2) _____ (hang) heavily, and there was a rawness in the air that suggested snow. A woman servant came into a room in which a child (3) _____ (sleep) and (4) _____ (draw) the curtains. She glanced mechanically at the house opposite, a stucco house with a portico, and went to the child's bed.

"Wake up, Philip," she said.

She pulled down the bed-clothes, took him in her arms, and carried him downstairs. He was only half awake.

"Your mother (5) _____ (want) you," she said.

She opened the door of a room on the floor below and took the child over to a bed in which a woman (6) _____ (lie). It was his mother. She stretched out her arms, and the child nestled by her side. He did not ask why he (7) _____ (awake). The woman kissed his eyes, and with thin, small hands felt the warm body through his white flannel nightgown. She pressed him closer to herself.

"(8) _____ (be) you sleepy, darling?" she said.

Her voice (9) _____ (be) so weak that it seemed to come already from a great distance. The child did not answer, but smiled comfortably. He was very happy in the large, warm bed, with those soft arms about him. He tried to make himself smaller still as he (10) _____ (cuddle) up against his mother, and he kissed her sleepily. In a moment he closed his eyes and was fast asleep. The doctor came forward

TIPS

past perfect past

PAST   NOW   FUTURE

and stood by the bed-side.

"Oh, don't take him away yet," she moaned.

The doctor, without (11) _____ (answer), looked at her gravely. Knowing she would not be allowed to keep the child much longer, the woman kissed him again; and she passed her hand down his body till she came to his feet; she held the right foot in her hand and felt the five small toes; and then slowly passed her hand over the left one. She gave a sob.

"What's the matter?" said the doctor. "You're tired."

She shook her head, unable to speak, and the tears rolled down her cheeks. The doctor (12) _____ (bend) down.

"Let me take him."

She was too weak to resist his wish, and she gave the child up. The doctor handed him back to his nurse.

"You'd better put him back in his own bed."

"Very well, sir." The little boy, still sleeping, was taken away. His mother sobbed now broken-heartedly.

"What (13) _____ (happen) to him, poor child?"

The monthly nurse tried to quiet her, and presently, from exhaustion, the crying ceased. The doctor walked to a table on the other side of the room, upon which, under a towel, lay the body of a

still-born child. He lifted the towel and looked. He was hidden from the bed by a screen, but the woman guessed what he was doing.

"Was it a girl or a boy?" she whispered to the nurse.

"Another boy."

The woman did not answer. In a moment the child's nurse came back. She approached the bed.

"Master Philip never (14) _____ (wake) up," she said. There was a pause. Then the doctor felt his patient's pulse once more.

"I don't think there's anything I can do just now," he said. "I (15) _____ (call) again after breakfast."

"I'll show you out, sir," said the child's nurse.

IV

Sister Carrie by Theodore Dreiser

When Caroline Meeber (1) _____ (board) the afternoon train for Chicago, her total outfit (2) _____ (consist) of a small trunk, a cheap imitation alligator-skin satchel, a small lunch in a paper box, and a yellow leather snap purse, (3) _____ (contain) her ticket, a scrap of paper with her sister's address in Van Buren Street, and four dollars in money. It was in August, 1889. She (4) _____ (be) was eighteen years of age, bright, timid, and full of the illusions of ignorance and youth. Whatever touch of regret at (5) _____ (part) characterised her thoughts, it was certainly not for advantages now being given up. A gush of tears at her mother's farewell kiss, a touch in her throat when the cars clacked by the flour mill where her father worked by the day, a pathetic sigh as the familiar green environs of the village passed in review, and the threads which (6) _____ (bind) her so lightly to girlhood and home (7) _____ (be) irretrievably broken.

To be sure there was always the next station, where one might descend and (8) _____ (return). There was the great city, bound more closely by these very trains which (9) _____ (come) up daily. Columbia City was not so very far away, even once she was in Chicago. What, pray, is a few hours — a few hundred miles? She looked at the little slip (10) _____ (bear) her sister's address and wondered. She gazed at the green landscape, now (11) _____ (pass) in swift review, until her swifter thoughts replaced its impression with vague conjectures of what Chicago (12) _____ (may) be.

When a girl (13) _____ (leave) her home at eighteen, she (14) _____ (do) one of two things. Either she (15) _____ (fall) into saving hands and (16) _____ (become) better, or she rapidly (17) _____ (assume) the cosmopolitan standard of virtue and (18) _____ (become) worse. Of an intermediate balance, under the circumstances, there is no possibility. The city has its cunning wiles, no less than the infinitely smaller and more human tempter. There (19) _____ (be) large forces which allure with all the soulfulness of expression possible in the most cultured human. The gleam of a thousand lights is often as effective as the persuasive light in a wooing and fascinating eye. Half the undoing of the unsophisticated and natural mind is accomplished by forces wholly superhuman. A blare of sound, a roar of life, a vast array of human hives, (20) _____ (appeal) to the astonished senses in equivocal terms. Without a counsellor at hand to whisper cautious interpretations, what falsehoods may not these things (21) _____(breathe) into the unguarded ear! Unrecognised for what they (22) _____ (be), their beauty, like music, too often (23) _____ (relax), then (24)_____ (weaken), then (25) _____ (pervert) the simpler human perceptions.

TIPS

ALWAYS

V

The Happy Prince by Oscar Wilde

"Who are you?" he said.

"I (1) _____ (be) the Happy Prince."

"Why are you weeping then?" asked the Swallow; "you (2) _____ (drench) me."

"When I (3) _____ (be) alive and (4) _____ (have) a human heart," answered the statue, "I did not know what tears were, for I lived in the Palace of Sans-Souci, where sorrow (5) _____ (be) not allowed to enter. In the daytime I played with my companions in the garden, and in the evening I led the dance in the Great Hall. Round the garden (6) _____ (run) a very lofty wall, but I never (7) _____ (care) to ask what lay beyond it, everything about me was so beautiful. My courtiers called me the Happy Prince, and happy indeed I was, if pleasure be happiness. So I lived, and so I died. And now that I (8) _____ (be) dead.

They (9) _____ (set) me up here so high that I can see all the ugliness and all the misery of my city, and though my heart is made of lead yet I cannot choose but (10) _____ (weep)."

TIPS

ALWAYS

"What! (11) _____ (be) he not solid gold?" said the Swallow to himself. He was too polite to make any personal remarks out loud.

"Far away," continued the statue in a low musical voice, "far away in a little street there is a poor house. One of the windows is open, and through it I can see a woman (12) _____ (seat) at a table. Her face is thin and worn, and she has coarse, red hands, all pricked by the needle, for she is a seamstress. She (13) _____ (embroider) passion−flowers on a satin

gown for the loveliest of the Queen's maids-of-honour to wear at the next Court-ball. In a bed in the corner of the room her little boy (14) _____ (lie) ill. He has a fever, and (15) _____ (ask) for oranges. His mother has nothing to give him but river water, so he (16) _____ (cry).

Swallow, Swallow, little Swallow, will you not bring her the ruby out of my sword-hilt? My feet are fastened to this pedestal and I cannot move."

"I am waited for in Egypt," said the Swallow. "My friends are flying up and down the Nile, and talking to the large lotus−flowers. Soon they (17) _____ (go) to sleep in the tomb of the great King. The King is there himself in his painted coffin. He is wrapped in yellow linen, and embalmed with spices. Round his neck is a chain of pale green jade, and his hands are like withered leaves."

"Swallow, Swallow, little Swallow," said the Prince, "will you not stay with me for one night, and be my messenger? The boy is so thirsty, and the mother so sad."

"I don't think I like boys," answered the Swallow. "Last summer, when I (18) _____ (stay) on the river, there were two rude boys, the miller's sons, who were always throwing stones at me. They never (19) _____ (hit) me, of course; we swallows (20) _____ (fly) far too well for that, and besides, I come of a family famous for its agility; but still, it (21) _____ (be) a mark of disrespect."

But the Happy Prince looked so sad that the little Swallow was sorry. "It is very cold here," he said; "but I (22) _____ (stay) with you for one night, and be your messenger."

"Thank you, little Swallow," said the Prince.

So the Swallow picked out the great ruby from the Prince's sword, and flew away with it in his beak over the roofs of the town.

VI

The Invisible Man by H. G. Wells

The stranger came early in February, one wintry day, through a biting wind and a driving snow, the last snowfall of the year, over the down, (1) _____ (walk) from Bramblehurst railway station, and (2) _____ (carry) a little black portmanteau in his thickly gloved hand. He was wrapped up from head to foot, and the brim of his soft felt hat (3) _____ (hide) every inch of his face but the shiny tip of his nose; the snow (4) _____ (pile) itself against his shoulders and chest, and (5) _____ (add) a white crest to the burden he carried. He staggered into the "Coach and Horses" more dead than alive, and (6) _____ (fling) his portmanteau down. "A fire," he cried, "in the name of human charity! A room and a fire!" He stamped and (7) _____ (shake) the snow from off himself in the bar, and followed Mrs. Hall into her guest parlour (8) _____ (strike) his bargain. And with that much introduction, that and a couple of sovereigns flung upon the table, he took up his quarters in the inn.

Mrs. Hall (9) _____ (light) the fire and left him there while she went to prepare him a meal with her own hands. A guest to stop in the wintertime (10) _____ (be) an unheard-of piece of luck, let alone a guest who was no "haggler," and she was resolved to show herself worthy of her good fortune. As soon as the bacon (11) _____ (be) well under way, and Millie, her lymphatic aid, (12) _____ (brisk) up a bit by a few deftly chosen expressions of contempt, she carried the cloth, plates, and glasses into the parlour and began to lay them with the utmost eclat.

Although the fire (13) _____ (burn) up briskly, she was surprised to

see that her visitor still (14) _____ his hat and

coat, (15) _____ (stand) with his back to her

and (16) _____ (stare) out of the window at the

(17) _____ (fall) snow in the yard. His gloved

hands were clasped behind him, and he seemed to

be lost in thought. She noticed that the melting snow

that still (18) _____ (sprinkle) his shoulders (19) _____ (drip)

upon her carpet. "Can I take your hat and coat, sir?" she said, "and (20)

_____ (give) them a good dry in the kitchen?"

"No," he said without turning.

She was not sure she (21) _____ (hear) him, and was about to

repeat her question.

VII

Why I write by George Orwell

From a very early age, perhaps the age of five or six, I knew that when I grew up I should be a writer. Between the ages of about seventeen and twenty-four I tried to abandon this idea, but I did so with the consciousness that I (1) _____ (outrage) my true nature and that sooner or later I should have to settle down and write books.

I (2) _____ (be) the middle child of three, but there was a gap of five years on either side, and I barely (3) _____ (see) my father before I was eight. For this and other reasons I was somewhat lonely, and I soon (4) _____ (develop) disagreeable mannerisms which (5) _____ (make) me unpopular throughout my schooldays. I had the lonely child's habit of making up stories and holding conversations with imaginary persons, and I (6)_____ (think) from the very start my literary ambitions (7) _____ (mix) up with the feeling of being isolated and undervalued. I (8) _____ (know) that I had a facility with words and a power of facing unpleasant facts, and I felt that this created a sort of private world in which I could get my own back for my failure in everyday life. Nevertheless the volume of serious – i.e. seriously intended – writing which I produced all through my childhood and boyhood (9) _____ not _____ (amount) to half a dozen pages.

I (10) _____ (write) my first poem at the age of four or five, my

mother taking it down to dictation. I (11) _____ (remember) anything

about it except that it was about a tiger and the tiger

had 'chair-like teeth' – a good enough phrase, but I

(12) _____ (fancy) the poem was a plagiarism

of Blake's 'Tiger, Tiger'. At eleven, when the war or

1914-18 (13) _____ (break) out, I wrote a

patriotic poem which (14) _____ (print)

in the local newspaper, as was another, two

years later, on the death of Kitchener. From

time to time, when I was a bit older, I wrote bad and usually unfinished

'nature poems' in the Georgian style. I also (15) _____ (attempt) a

short story which was a ghastly failure. That was the total of the would-be

serious work that I actually (16) _____ (set) down on paper during all

those years.

時態是相對的。用甚麼時態，
可以不止一個選擇。

創意寫作：看漫畫，寫故事，想時態
Creative Writing Exercises

Exercise 01

Buying shoes

請按每格的提示文字，用正確時態寫出故事

buy, fashionable, famous

show off, admire

feel, uncomfortable shoes

complain, can't walk,
have to walk

Exercise 02

Moms are everywhere

請按每格的提示文字，用正確時態寫出故事。

go, shopping, supermarket

lose, run, yell, aisles

find, scold, call, should

reply, know, find

Exercise 03

The man who charges whenever you talk with him

請按每格的提示文字，用正確時態寫出故事

lawyer, drive, new Ferrari

lose, come, drive

say, panic, tremble, fear

wave, run, charge, frightened

Exercise 04

How to get your life insured

請按每格的提示文字，用正確時態寫出故事。

insure, die

heart attack, brain cancer

reject, apply, life insurance

go, insure, ask

tell, die

agree, insure

進階—虛擬時態

來到這章，你是否有信心正確運用時態呢？

其實，在英文世界中，還有一些貌似時態的文法要多加留意。

⊕ **先看以下幾個例子：**

If John were rich, he would buy a new flat.

I am going to see the doctor next Monday.

She was afraid of seeing his mother.

⊕ **問題來了：**

would 看來像過去式，是指已發生的事嗎？

am going to 明明是現在進行式，與將來有關嗎？

was afraid of 之後的 seeing 是指這個動作正在進行嗎？

以下將為你一一解答。

5.1 虛擬語氣
Subjunctive mood —— 用 were 卻不是過去式

- If I were rich, I would travel round the world.
- If Jenny were to be reborn, she would be a singer.

虛擬語氣用 were 及 would + 動詞，看起來像過去式，但它並非時態，時間上也不是指過去，而是指現在，表示與現在發生的事實不符。

- If John were rich, he would buy a new flat. （現在沒有錢）
- If you were here, you could give him good advice. （現在不在場）

were 之後加 to，可指與未來發生的事實相反的假設。

- If the sun were to rise in the west, Peter would not change his mind. （太陽絕不可能從西邊升起）

注意，表達與未來事實不符，不管是第一、二或三人稱，也不管是單數或複數，都用 were to 加動詞原形。

➕ 5.1.1 辨別虛擬時態 were

⊕ 注意虛擬時態 were 的提示詞：
虛擬時態 were 前面一般有一些特別的提示詞，如 wish, if, as if。

- I wish the meeting were over. （會議還沒有結束）
- If I were you, I would tell him the truth. （我不是你）
- Tom talks as if he were a boss. （Tom 不是老闆）

⊕ 注意虛擬時態 were 之前的主語：
過去式的 were 只用於主語 we, you, they，當主語是 I 或 he, she, it，不用 were 而用 was。但在虛擬時態的 were，不管主語是甚麼人稱都可以用 were。

- If I were you, I would accept the offer.
- If he/she were in Hong Kong, I would arrange a meeting with him/her.
- If it were to be considered, I would be grateful.

5.1.2 虛擬語氣 Subjunctive mood —— 用 had + 過去分詞卻不是過去完成式

If I had saved more money, I would have travelled around the world.

虛擬語氣用 had + 過去分詞，看起來像過去完成式，但它並非時態，時間上也不是指在過去某一時間之前完成的動作，而是表示與 "過去" 發生的事實不符。

- If Paul had studied hard, he could have passed the final exam.（保羅沒有用功讀書）
- If I had had more time, I would have helped you finish the project.（我沒有更多時間）

5.1.3 辨別虛擬時態 had + 過去分詞

注意虛擬時態 "had + 過去分詞" 的提示詞：

虛擬時態 had + 過去分詞前面一般有一些特別的提示詞，如 wish, if, if only.

I wish I had studied hard. I failed my final exam.（回想以前，希望能改變）

If only I had not quarrelled with my mother.（回想以前，表示遺憾）

而過去完成式的提示詞，如 before, after，是用來表示一個動作已經發生在另一個過去動作之前。

After I had finished reading my book, I put out the light.（關燈之前我已讀了書）

I had left the office before he arrived.（他來之前我已離開辦公室）

5.2 動名詞
Gerund —— 有 -ing 卻不是進行式

I consider finding a new house.

Gerund 表面上和進行式一樣，都是動詞加 -ing，但它不是時態，而是像它的名稱一樣，由動詞變成名詞。

因為變成了名詞，所以 Gerund 可以做主詞或者做受詞。

Gerund 在文法上的功能像形容詞，表示狀態或動作，也可以表示已經發生的動作。

➕ 5 2 1 辨別動名詞

⊕ **注意動名詞的提示詞：**

動名詞前面一般有一些特別動詞，如 appreciate, avoid, consider, enjoy, escape, finish, imagine, mind, miss, practice, quit 等。

- I enjoy playing football.
- Paul quitted smoking when his son was born.
- The little boy tried to escape punishment by putting the blame on his little sister.

⊕ **動名詞的動作沒有進行中的意思：**

它是表示動作這回事，沒有特別的時間，如果有時間因素，那麼也是已經完成的。

- Playing basketball is Tom's hobby. （Tom 喜歡打籃球，但他不一定正在打籃球）
- Sam often goes swimming in a beach. （go swimming 的 swimming 形容游泳的動作，Sam 經常去海灘游泳，但他在這一刻不一定是在游泳。）
- Stop complaining, please. （已開始埋怨）
- I forgot calling my brother. （忘記打電話這事已發生了）

想知道以上例句裏，go 之後為何不用 to swim，forget 之後為何不用 to call my brother, 請參看下文。

➕ 5.2.2 比較動名詞和不定詞 infinitive

在動詞之後，用動名詞或不定詞，表達的意思不同。

用動名詞表示動作已經發生，用不定詞表示動作還沒發生。

I forgot telling him the good news. (我忘了（我）已把好消息告訴了他。)

I forgot to tell him the good news. (我忘了告訴他這個好消息。)

有幾個常見動詞，如 stop, forget, remember, regret 等可用動名詞或

不定詞以表達不同意思。

➕ 5.2.3 比較動名詞和現在分詞

➕ 動名詞表示"性質"或者"用途"：

• Jimmy travelled around Europe by his sleeping car.

• Sam would rather go swimming in a beach than a swimming pool.

這兩句裏，his sleeping car, a swimming pool 都是動名詞，表示 car

的用途是供 Jimmy 睡覺；a swimming pool 的用途是游泳。

➕ 現在分詞的功能像形容詞，表示狀態或動作：

• Janet kissed her sleeping son.

• The children were very excited to see two swimming dolphins at the
beach.

這兩個例句裏，her sleeping son, swimming dolphins 都是現在分

詞，形容 Janet 的兒子正在睡覺，海豚正在游泳。

5.3 現在進行式 ── 不是表示正在進行的動作

I am going to see the doctor next Monday.

前面學過現在進行式用來表示正在進行的動作，但其實它還有其他用途，可以與現在沒有關係，而是表示安排在將來要做的事情。

例 | • Are you coming to the birthday party tonight? （詢問你是否會來）
注意，遇到這種情況，也可以用將來式。

例 | • Will you come to the birthday party tonight?

➕ 5.3.1 辨別現在進行式的用法

現在進行式表示正在進行的動作時，一般有提示詞如 when, while 等。而表示將要發生的事，一般有提示詞如 next week, tomorrow 等。如果沒有提示詞，從上文下理也可以判斷事情是不是正在進行。

 | • I am not asking John to the party. （派對還未開始）

➕ 5.3.2 例外情況──不用現在進行式表示將來

當我們預測或報導一些活動或事情，而它們不在我們的控制範圍之內，也不能讓我們隨意安排，不能用現在進行式，要用將來式。

 | • Scientists say that more tropical storms will come this summer.
| • The rainforests in Brazil will disappear soon if nothing is done to preserve them.

在表示將來恆常的情況時，不用現在進行式，要用將來式。

例 | • People will face more and more health problems in the future.
| • The new exhibition hall will have ten conference rooms.

時態這回事，拿着時態總圖
表，多讀文章多揣摩，你一定
可以掌握。

附錄：不規則動詞表
Appendix : List of Irregular Verbs

注意：用斜線號分開不同拼寫形式。最常用的排在前面。

動詞原形	過去式	過去分詞
A		
arise	arose	arisen
awake	awoke	awaken
B		
backslide	backslid	backslidden / backslid
be	was, were	been
bear	bore	borne
beat	beat	beaten
become	became	become
begin	began	begun
bend	bent	bent
bet	bet	bet
bid (bid someone goodbye /good evening)	bid / bade	bidden
bid (bid for sth by offering a particular amount of money)	bid	bid
bind	bound	bound
bite	bit	bitten
bleed	bled	bled

動詞原形	過去式	過去分詞
blow	blew	blown
break	broke	broken
breed	bred	bred
bring	brought	brought
broadcast	broadcast	broadcast
browbeat	browbeat	browbeaten
build	built	built
burn	burnt	burnt
burst	burst	burst
bust	bust	bust
buy	bought	bought
C		
cast	cast	cast
catch	caught	caught
choose	chose	chosen
cling	clung	clung
come	came	come
cost	cost	cost
creep	crept	crept
crossbreed	crossbred	crossbred
cut	cut	cut
D		
daydream	daydreamt	daydreamt

動詞原形	過去式	過去分詞
deal	dealt	dealt
dig	dug	dug
disprove	disproved	disproven
dive (jump head-first)	dove / dived	dived
dive (scuba diving)	dived / dove	dived
do	did	done
draw	drew	drawn
dream	dreamt	dreamt
drink	drank	drunk
drive	drove	driven
dwell	dwelt	dwelt
	E	
eat	ate	eaten
	F	
fall	fell	fallen
feed	fed	fed
feel	felt	felt
fight	fought	fought
find	found	found
fit (tailor, change size)	fitted/fit	fitted/fit
fit (be right size)	fit/fitted	fit/fitted
flee	fled	fled
fling	flung	flung

動詞原形	過去式	過去分詞
fly	flew	flown
forbid	forbade	forbidden
forecast	forecast	forecast
forego (also forgo)	forewent	foregone
foresee	foresaw	foreseen
foretell	foretold	foretold
forget	forgot	forgotten
forgive	forgave	forgiven
forsake	forsook	forsaken
freeze	froze	frozen
frostbite	frostbit	frostbitten
G		
get	got	gotten/got
give	gave	given
go	went	gone
grind	ground	ground
grow	grew	grown
H		
hand-feed	hand-fed	hand-fed
handwrite	handwrote	handwritten
hang	hung	hung
have	had	had
hear	heard	heard

動詞原形	過去式	過去分詞
hew	hewed	hewn
hide	hid	hidden
hit	hit	hit
hold	held	held
hurt	hurt	hurt
I		
inbreed	inbred	inbred
inlay	inlaid	inlaid
input	input	input
interbreed	interbred	interbred
interweave	interwove	interwoven
interwind	interwound	interwound
J		
jerry-build	jerry-built	jerry-built
K		
keep	kept	kept
kneel	knelt	knelt
knit	knit	knit
know	knew	known
L		
lay	laid	laid
lead	led	led
lean	leant	leant

動詞原形	過去式	過去分詞
leap	leapt	leapt
learn	learnt	learnt
leave	left	left
lend	lent	lent
let	let	let
lie	lay	lain
lie (not tell truth) REGULAR	lied	lied
light	lit / lighted	lit / lighted
lip-read	lip-read	lip-read
lose	lost	lost
M		
make	made	made
mean	meant	meant
meet	met	met
miscast	miscast	miscast
misdeal	misdealt	misdealt
misdo	misdid	misdone
mishear	misheard	misheard
mislay	mislaid	mislaid
mislead	misled	misled
mislearn	mislearnt	mislearnt
misread	misread	misread
misset	misset	misset

動詞原形	過去式	過去分詞
misspeak	misspoke	misspoken
misspell	misspelt	misspelt
misspend	misspent	misspent
mistake	mistook	mistaken
misteach	mistaught	mistaught
misunderstand	misunderstood	misunderstood
miswrite	miswrote	miswritten
mow	mowed	mown
O		
offset	offset	offset
outbid	outbid	outbid
outbreed	outbred	outbred
outdo	outdid	outdone
outdraw	outdrew	outdrawn
outdrink	outdrank	outdrunk
outdrive	outdrove	outdriven
outfight	outfought	outfought
outfly	outflew	outflown
outgrow	outgrew	outgrown
outleap	outleapt	outleapt
outlie (not tell truth) REGULAR	outlied	outlied
outride	outrode	outridden

動詞原形	過去式	過去分詞
outrun	outran	outrun
outsell	outsold	outsold
outshine	outshone	outshone
outshoot	outshot	outshot
outsing	outsang	outsung
outsit	outsat	outsat
outsleep	outslept	outslept
outsmell	outsmelt	outsmelt
outspeak	outspoke	outspoken
outspeed	outsped	outsped
outspend	outspent	outspent
outswear	outswore	outsworn
outswim	outswam	outswum
outthink	outthought	outthought
outthrow	outthrew	outthrown
outwrite	outwrote	outwritten
overbid	overbid	overbid
overbreed	overbred	overbred
overbuild	overbuilt	overbuilt
overbuy	overbought	overbought
overcome	overcame	overcome
overdo	overdid	overdone
overdraw	overdrew	overdrawn

動詞原形	過去式	過去分詞
overdrink	overdrank	overdrunk
overeat	overate	overeaten
overfeed	overfed	overfed
overhang	overhung	overhung
overhear	overheard	overheard
overlay	overlaid	overlaid
overpay	overpaid	overpaid
override	overrode	overridden
overrun	overran	overrun
oversee	oversaw	overseen
oversell	oversold	oversold
oversew	oversewed	oversewn
overshoot	overshot	overshot
oversleep	overslept	overslept
overspeak	overspoke	overspoken
overspend	overspent	overspent
overspill	overspilt	overspilt
overtake	overtook	overtaken
overthink	overthought	overthought
overthrow	overthrew	overthrown
overwind	overwound	overwound
overwrite	overwrote	overwritten

動詞原形	過去式	過去分詞
	P	
partake	partook	partaken
pay	paid	paid
plead	pleaded / pled	pleaded / pled
prebuild	prebuilt	prebuilt
predo	predid	predone
premake	premade	premade
prepay	prepaid	prepaid
presell	presold	presold
preset	preset	preset
preshrink	preshrank	preshrunk
proofread	proofread	proofread
prove	proved	proven
put	put	put
	Q	
quick-freeze	quick-froze	quick-frozen
quit	quit/quitted	quit/quitted
	R	
read	read (sounds like "red")	read (sounds like "red")
reawake	reawoke	reawaken
rebid	rebid	rebid
rebind	rebound	rebound

動詞原形	過去式	過去分詞
rebroadcast	rebroadcast / rebroadcasted	rebroadcast / rebroadcasted
rebuild	rebuilt	rebuilt
recast	recast	recast
recut	recut	recut
redeal	redealt	redealt
redo	redid	redone
redraw	redrew	redrawn
refit (replace parts)	refit/refitted	refit/refitted
refit (retailor)	refitted/refit	refitted/refit
regrind	reground	reground
regrow	regrew	regrown
rehang	rehung	rehung
rehear	reheard	reheard
reknit	reknitted / reknit	reknitted / reknit
relay (for example tiles)	relaid	relaid
relay (pass along) REGULAR	relayed	relayed
relearn	relearnt	relearnt
relight	relit / relighted	relit / relighted
remake	remade	remade
repay	repaid	repaid
reread	reread	reread
rerun	reran	rerun

動詞原形	過去式	過去分詞
resell	resold	resold
resend	resent	resent
reset	reset	reset
resew	resewed	resewn
retake	retook	retaken
reteach	retaught	retaught
retear	retore	retorn
retell	retold	retold
rethink	rethought	rethought
retread	retread	retread
retrofit	retrofitted/retrofit	retrofitted/retrofit
rewake	rewoke	rewaken
rewear	rewore	reworn
reweave	rewove	rewoven
rewed	rewed / rewedded	rewed / rewedded
rewet	rewet/rewetted	rewet/rewetted
rewin	rewon	rewon
rewind	rewound	rewound
rewrite	rewrote	rewritten
rid	rid	rid
ride	rode	ridden
ring	rang	rung
rise	rose	risen

動詞原形	過去式	過去分詞
roughcast	roughcast	roughcast
run	ran	run
	S	
sand-cast	sand-cast	sand-cast
saw	sawed	sawn
say	said	said
see	saw	seen
seek	sought	sought
sell	sold	sold
send	sent	sent
set	set	set
sew	sewed	sewn
shake	shook	shaken
shave	shaved	shaven
shear	sheared	shorn
shed	shed	shed
shine	shone	shone
shit	shit / *shat* / shitted	shit/ *shat* / shitted
shoot	shot	shot
show	showed	shown
shrink	shrank	shrunk
shut	shut	shut
sight-read	sight-read	sight-read

動詞原形	過去式	過去分詞
sing	sang	sung
sink	sank	sunk
sit	sat	sat
slay (kill)	slew	slain
slay (amuse) REGULAR	slayed	slayed
sleep	slept	slept
slide	slid	slid
sling	slung	slung
slink	slunk	slunk
slit	slit	slit
smell	smelt	smelt
sneak	snuck	snuck
sow	sowed	sown
speak	spoke	spoken
speed	sped	sped
spell	spelt	spelt
spend	spent	spent
spill	spilt	spilt
spin	spun	spun
spit	spit / *spat*	spit / *spat*
split	split	split
spoil	spoilt	spoilt
spoon-feed	spoon-fed	spoon-fed

動詞原形	過去式	過去分詞
spread	spread	spread
spring	sprang	sprung
stand	stood	stood
steal	stole	stolen
stick	stuck	stuck
sting	stung	stung
stink	stank	stunk
strew	strewed	strewn
stride	strode	stridden
strike (delete)	struck	stricken
strike (hit)	struck	stricken
string	strung	strung
strive	strove	striven
sublet	sublet	sublet
sunburn	sunburnt	sunburnt
swear	swore	sworn
sweat	sweat	sweat
sweep	swept	swept
swell	swelled	swollen
swim	swam	swum
swing	swung	swung
T		
take	took	taken

動詞原形	過去式	過去分詞
teach	taught	taught
tear	tore	torn
telecast	telecast	telecast
tell	told	told
test-drive	test-drove	test-driven
test-fly	test-flew	test-flown
think	thought	thought
throw	threw	thrown
thrust	thrust	thrust
tread	trod	trodden
typecast	typecast	typecast
typeset	typeset	typeset
typewrite	typewrote	typewritten
U		
unbend	unbent	unbent
unbind	unbound	unbound
unclothe	unclothed/unclad	unclothed/unclad
underbid	underbid	underbid
undercut	undercut	undercut
underfeed	underfed	underfed
undergo	underwent	undergone
underlie	underlay	underlain
undersell	undersold	undersold

動詞原形	過去式	過去分詞
underspend	underspent	underspent
understand	understood	understood
undertake	undertook	undertaken
underwrite	underwrote	underwritten
undo	undid	undone
unfreeze	unfroze	unfrozen
unhang	unhung	unhung
unhide	unhid	unhidden
unknit	unknitted/unknit	unknitted/unknit
unlearn	unlearnt	unlearnt
unsew	unsewed	unsewn
unsling	unslung	unslung
unspin	unspun	unspun
unstick	unstuck	unstuck
unstring	unstrung	unstrung
unweave	unwove	unwoven
unwind	unwound	unwound
uphold	upheld	upheld
upset	upset	upset
W		
wake	woke	woken
waylay	waylaid	waylaid
wear	wore	worn

動詞原形	過去式	過去分詞
weave	wove	woven
wed	wed / wedded	wed / wedded
weep	wept	wept
wet	wet/wetted	wet/wetted
win	won	won
wind	wound	wound
withdraw	withdrew	withdrawn
withhold	withheld	withheld
withstand	withstood	withstood
wring	wrung	wrung
write	wrote	written

Ⅰ 填空題

1 were waiting, ran

2 was dead

3 went, had made

4 finished, left

5 are having, get / were having, got

6 have been waiting

7 had been raining

8 had left

9 had given

10 will be doing

11 will have pulled down

12 did, had been

13 have painted, moved / had painted, move

14 Do

15 travels

16 am calling, comes / was calling, came

17 has made, died / had made, died

18 had worked

19 saw, occurred, crossed

20 stopped, began

21 was, were playing

22 shall / will have been stuying

23 shall / will have saved

24 did, get

25 will have studied / will have been studying

26 failed, have made

27 said, had read

28 turned off, went

29 will be

30 will have settled

31 were testing, went

32 have been

33 was

34 made

35 told, moved

36 was putting, rang

37 jumped, was moving

38 Did, go

39 was reading, was plying, heard

40 had been

41 were not

42 is reading, is playing / was reading, was playing

43 are getting /, shall / will get

44 have studied, left

45 had run away, arrived

46 will have repaired

47 am showing / will be showing

48 am seeing / will be seeing

49 had done

50 had been, went

51 was, reached, was sitting, were lying, was bending

52 have read

53 did not want, were working

54 was, had thought

55 finished

56 was walking, began

57 shall / will have learnt

58 will have finished

59 arrived, had left

60 did not tell

61 (1) will have been living

(2) will have been teaching

(3) will leave

(4) will be taking

(5) will be enjoying

(6) will come

(7) will be working

(8) will have finished

II 畫以下句子的正確 timeline

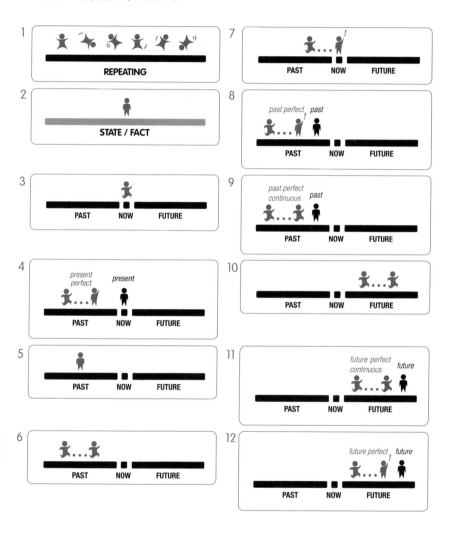

III 選擇題

1 B 2 A 3 C 4 C 5 D 6 C 7 D 8 D 9 C 10 B 11 B 12 C 13 C 14 C
15 D 16 C 17 B 18 A 19 A 20 A

IV 翻譯以下句子

1 He came in when we have just finished our breakfast.

2 I will have finished reading this novel by next Wednesday.

3 When he came in, I had been tryiny hard to fix the television set for several hours.

4 I think little baby would be sound asleep by the time Mom went home.

5 The road became a danger at that time. It had teen raining for 2 days.

6 The plane would take off before we could get to the airport.

7 The boy was very happy with his new bike. He had hoped for it for a long time.

8 Tomorrow at this time she will be in Paris.

9 By the time we reached the mountain peak, the sun had already risen.

10 Next year my parents will have been married for 31 years.

V 句型轉換

1 I had not sold the ticket before she arrived.

2 She did not sing a song to us when she danced.

3 They did not begin to climb the mountain until they had bought all the food.

4 Will John have been hungry by 10:00 a.m.?

5 Had Lucy completed the project when Mike arrived?

6 By the time he got to the airport, had the plane taken off?

7 What had happened to him when I saw him?

8 Where did he go after he had read the note?

9 Why didn't Jack go to the cinema?

10 How long had we had the toys before we gave them away?

11 What had she written by the end of 1960?

12 After we had cooked the dumplings, we ate them up.

13 After the car had broden, Jim's father repaired it.

14 After we had sat for our exams, we had a long holiday.

15 Before he showed us around the house, he had shown us a picture.

B 練習答案
Answer Key

I

An interview

Host: Senator Smith, (1) <u>thank</u> you for joining us.

Senator: Thank you so much for having me.

Host: The financial assets (2) <u>are shrinking</u>. Gasoline is above $3 a gallon. Tell us how your economic plan (3) <u>will take</u> us higher.

Senator: Well, (4) <u>it's going to start with</u> dealing with the immediate crisis, both in the financial markets and in the housing market. And obviously, those things (5) <u>are connected</u>.

On the housing market, I (6) <u>think</u> it is important for us to create some bottom, giving people some sense of where this (7) <u>will end</u>. The government should (8) <u>step</u> in to help stabilize the market. It's not a bailout for borrowers or lenders, but what it (9) <u>says</u> is we (10) <u>will rework</u> some of these loan packages so that they're affordable. And, you know, everybody's going to have to take a haircut, the borrowers and the lenders, but it won't be as bad as if a foreclosure took place.

Step number two, I think we (11) <u>will stabilize</u> and (12) <u>provide</u> confidence in the financial markets. It is important to make sure that we (13) <u>have coupled</u> that with some new regulatory structures.

The third thing is to understand that the economy has been out of balance for quite some time. We (14) <u>had</u> high corporate profits, enormous rises in productivity over the last decade but wages and incomes (15) <u>have flat-lined</u>. And so you (16) <u>had</u> a lot of concentrated wealth at the top, but ordinary folks (17) <u>were hammered</u> with rising gas prices, rising costs of health care, rising costs of college tuition.

And so creating a tax code that is more equitable and making sure that we (18) <u>are making</u> investments in things like infrastructure and clean energy can put us on a more stable long-term competitive footing. I think that has to be part of the package as well.

II

You and the atomic bomb by George Orwell

We were once told that the aeroplane (1) <u>had abolished</u> frontiers; actually it is only since the aeroplane became a serious weapon that frontiers (2) <u>have become</u> definitely impassable. The radio was once expected to promote international understanding and co-operation; it (3) <u>has turned</u> out to be a means of insulating one nation from another. The atomic bomb may complete the process by robbing the exploited classes and peoples of all power to revolt, and at the same time putting the possessors of the bomb on a basis of military equality. Unable to conquer one another, they are likely to continue ruling the world between them, and it is difficult to see how the balance can be upset except by slow and unpredictable demographic changes.

For forty or fifty years past, Mr. H.G. Wells and others (4) <u>have been warning</u> us that man is in danger of destroying himself with his own weapons, leaving the ants or some other gregarious species to take over. Anyone who (5) <u>has seen</u> the ruined cities of Germany (6) <u>will find</u> this notion at least thinkable. Nevertheless, looking at the world as a whole, the drift for many decades (7) <u>has been</u> not towards anarchy but towards the reimposition of slavery. We may (8) <u>be heading</u> not for general breakdown but for an epoch as horribly stable as the slave empires of antiquity. James Burnham's theory (9) <u>has been</u> much <u>discussed</u>, but few people (10) <u>have</u> yet <u>considered</u> its ideological implications — that is, the kind of world-view, the kind of beliefs, and the social structure that (11) <u>would</u> probably <u>prevail</u> in a state which was at once unconquerable and in a permanent state of "cold war" with its neighbors.

III

Of human bondage by W. Somerset Maugham

The day (1) <u>broke</u> gray and dull. The clouds (2) <u>hung</u> heavily, and there was a rawness in the air that suggested snow. A woman servant came into a room in which a child (3) <u>was sleeping</u> and (4) <u>drew</u> the curtains. She glanced mechanically at the house opposite, a stucco house with a portico, and went to the child's bed.

"Wake up, Philip," she said.

She pulled down the bed-clothes, took him in her arms, and carried him downstairs. He was only half awake.

"Your mother (5) <u>wants</u> you," she said.

She opened the door of a room on the floor below and took the child over to a bed in which a woman (6) <u>was lying</u>. It was his mother. She stretched out her arms, and the child nestled by her side. He did not ask why he (7) <u>had been awakened</u>. The woman kissed his eyes, and with thin, small hands felt the warm body through his white flannel nightgown. She pressed him closer to herself.

"(8) <u>Are</u> you sleepy, darling?" she said.

Her voice (9) <u>was</u> so weak that it seemed to come already from a great distance. The child did not answer, but smiled comfortably. He was very happy in the large, warm bed, with those soft arms about him. He tried to make himself smaller still as he (10) <u>cuddled</u> up against his mother, and he kissed her sleepily. In a moment he closed his eyes and was fast asleep. The doctor came forwards and stood by the bed-side.

"Oh, don't take him away yet," she moaned.

The doctor, without (11) <u>answering</u>, looked at her gravely. Knowing she would not be allowed to keep the child much longer, the woman kissed him again; and she passed her hand down his body till she came to his feet; she held the right foot in her hand and felt the five small toes; and then slowly passed her hand over the left one. She gave a sob.

"What's the matter?" said the doctor. "You're tired."

She shook her head, unable to speak, and the tears rolled down her cheeks. The doctor (12) <u>bent</u> down.

"Let me take him."

She was too weak to resist his wish, and she gave the child up. The doctor handed him back to his nurse.

"You'd better put him back in his own bed."

"Very well, sir." The little boy, still sleeping, was taken away. His mother sobbed now broken-heartedly.

"What (13) <u>will happen</u> to him, poor child?"

The monthly nurse tried to quiet her, and presently, from exhaustion, the crying ceased. The doctor walked to a table on the other side of the room, upon which, under a towel, lay the body of a still-born child. He lifted the towel and looked. He was hidden from the bed by a screen, but the woman guessed what he was doing.

"Was it a girl or a boy?" she whispered to the nurse.

"Another boy."

The woman did not answer. In a moment the child's nurse came back. She approached the bed.

"Master Philip never (14) <u>woke</u> up," she said. There was a pause. Then the doctor felt his patient's pulse once more.

"I don't think there's anything I can do just now," he said. "I (15) <u>will call</u> again after breakfast."

"I'll show you out, sir," said the child's nurse.

IV

Sister Carrie by Theodore Dreiser

When Caroline Meeber (1) <u>boarded</u> the afternoon train for Chicago, her total outfit (2) <u>consisted</u> of a small trunk, a cheap imitation alligator-skin satchel, a small lunch in a paper box, and a yellow leather snap purse, (3) <u>containing</u> her ticket, a scrap of paper with her sister's address in Van Buren Street, and four dollars in money. It was in August, 1889. She (4) <u>was</u> eighteen years of age, bright, timid, and full of the illusions of ignorance and youth. Whatever touch of regret at (5) <u>parting</u> characterised her thoughts, it was certainly not for advantages now being given up. A gush of tears at her mother's farewell kiss, a touch in her throat when the cars clacked by the flour mill where her father worked by the day, a pathetic sigh as the familiar green environs of the village passed in review, and the threads which (6) <u>bound</u> her so lightly to girlhood and home (7) <u>were</u> irretrievably broken.

To be sure there was always the next station, where one might descend and (8) <u>return</u>. There was the great city, bound more closely by these very trains which (9) <u>came</u> up daily. Columbia City was not so very far away, even once she was in Chicago. What, pray, is a few hours – a few hundred miles? She looked at the little slip (10) <u>bearing</u> her sister's address and wondered. She gazed at the green landscape, now (11) <u>passing</u> in swift review, until her swifter thoughts replaced its impression with vague conjectures of what Chicago (12) <u>might</u> be.

When a girl (13) <u>leaves</u> her home at eighteen, she (14) <u>does</u> one of two things. Either she (15) <u>falls</u> into saving hands and (16) <u>becomes</u> better, or she rapidly (17) <u>assumes</u> the cosmopolitan standard of virtue and (18) <u>becomes</u> worse. Of an intermediate balance, under the circumstances, there is no possibility. The city has its cunning wiles, no less than the infinitely smaller and more human tempter. There (19) <u>are</u> large forces which allure with all the soulfulness of expression possible in the most cultured human. The gleam of a thousand lights is often as effective as the persuasive light in a wooing and fascinating eye. Half the undoing of the unsophisticated and natural mind is accomplished by forces wholly superhuman. A blare of sound, a roar of life, a vast array of human hives, (20) <u>appeal</u> to the astonished senses in equivocal terms. Without a counsellor at hand to whisper cautious interpretations, what falsehoods may not these things (21) <u>breathe</u> into the unguarded ear! Unrecognised for what they (22) <u>are</u>, their beauty, like music, too often (23) <u>relaxes</u>, then (24) <u>weakens</u>, then (25) <u>perverts</u> the simpler human perceptions.

V

The Happy Prince by Oscar Wilde

"Who are you?" he said.

"I (1) <u>am</u> the Happy Prince."

"Why are you weeping then?" asked the Swallow; "you (2) <u>drenched</u> me."

"When I (3) <u>was</u> alive and (4) <u>had</u> a human heart," answered the statue, "I did not know what tears were, for I lived in the Palace of Sans-Souci, where sorrow (5) <u>is</u> not allowed to enter. In the daytime I played with my companions in the garden, and in the evening I led the dance in the Great Hall. Round the garden (6) <u>ran</u> a very lofty wall, but I never (7) <u>cared</u> to ask what lay beyond it, everything about me was so beautiful. My courtiers called me the Happy Prince, and happy indeed I was, if pleasure be happiness. So I lived, and so I died. And now that I (8) <u>am</u> dead.

They (9) <u>have set</u> me up here so high that I can see all the ugliness and all the misery of my city, and though my heart is made of lead yet I cannot choose but (10) <u>weep</u>."

"What! (11) <u>Is</u> he not solid gold?" said the Swallow to himself. He was too polite to make any personal remarks out loud.

"Far away," continued the statue in a low musical voice, "far away in a little street there is a poor house. One of the windows is open, and through it I can see a woman (12) <u>seated</u> at a table. Her face is thin and worn, and she has coarse, red hands, all pricked by the needle, for she is a seamstress. She (13) <u>is embroidering</u> passion-flowers on a satin gown for the loveliest of the Queen's maids-of-honour to wear at the next Court-ball. In a bed in the corner of the room her little boy (14) <u>is lying</u> ill. He has a fever, and (15) <u>is asking</u> for oranges. His mother has nothing to give him but river water, so he (16) <u>is crying</u>.

Swallow, Swallow, little Swallow, will you not bring her the ruby out of my sword-hilt? My feet are fastened to this pedestal and I cannot move."

"I am waited for in Egypt," said the Swallow. "My friends are flying up and down the Nile, and talking to the large lotus-flowers. Soon they (17) <u>will go</u> to sleep in the tomb of the great King. The King is there himself in his painted coffin. He is wrapped in yellow linen, and embalmed with spices. Round his neck is a chain of pale green jade, and his hands are like withered leaves."

"Swallow, Swallow, little Swallow," said the Prince, "will you not stay with me for one night, and be my messenger? The boy is so thirsty, and the mother so sad."

"I don't think I like boys," answered the Swallow. "Last summer, when I (18) <u>was staying</u> on the river, there were two rude boys, the miller's sons, who were always throwing stones at me. They never (19) <u>hit</u> me, of course; we swallows (20) <u>fly</u> far too well for that, and besides, I come of a family famous for its agility; but still, it (21) <u>was</u> a mark of disrespect."

But the Happy Prince looked so sad that the little Swallow was sorry. "It is very cold here," he said; "but I (22) <u>will stay</u> with you for one night, and be your messenger."

"Thank you, little Swallow," said the Prince.

So the Swallow picked out the great ruby from the Prince's sword, and flew away with it in his beak over the roofs of the town.

<h1 style="text-align:center">VI</h1>

The Invisible Man by H. G. Wells

  The stranger came early in February, one wintry day, through a biting wind and a driving snow, the last snowfall of the year, over the down, (1) <u>walking</u> from Bramblehurst railway station, and (2) <u>carrying</u> a little black portmanteau in his thickly gloved hand. He was wrapped up from head to foot, and the brim of his soft felt hat (3) <u>hid</u> every inch of his face but the shiny tip of his nose; the snow (4) <u>had piled</u> itself against his shoulders and chest, and (5) <u>added</u> a white crest to the burden he carried. He staggered into the "Coach and Horses" more dead than alive, and (6) <u>flung</u> his portmanteau down. "A fire," he cried, "in the name of human charity! A room and a fire!" He stamped and (7) <u>shook</u> the snow from off himself in the bar, and followed Mrs. Hall into her guest parlour (8) <u>to strike</u> his bargain. And with that much introduction, that and a couple of sovereigns flung upon the table, he took up his quarters in the inn.

  Mrs. Hall (9) <u>lit</u> the fire and left him there while she went to prepare him a meal with her own hands. A guest to stop in the wintertime (10) <u>was</u> an unheard-of piece of luck, let alone a guest who was no "haggler," and she was resolved to show herself worthy of her good fortune. As soon as the bacon (11) <u>was</u> well under way, and Millie, her aid, (12) <u>had been brisked</u> up a bit by a few deftly chosen expressions of contempt, she carried the cloth, plates, and glasses into the parlour and began to lay them with the utmost eclat. Although the fire (13) <u>was burning</u> up briskly, she was surprised to see that her visitor still (14) <u>wore</u> his hat and coat, (15) <u>standing</u> with his back to her and (16) <u>staring</u> out of the window at the (17) <u>falling</u> snow in the yard. His gloved hands were clasped behind him, and he seemed to be lost in thought. She noticed that the melting snow that still (18) <u>sprinkled</u> his shoulders (19) <u>dripped</u> upon her carpet. "Can I take your hat and coat, sir?" she said, "and (20) <u>give</u> them a good dry in the kitchen?"

  "No," he said without turning.

  She was not sure she (21) <u>had heard</u> him, and was about to repeat her question.

VII

Why I write by George Orwell

From a very early age, perhaps the age of five or six, I knew that when I grew up I should be a writer. Between the ages of about seventeen and twenty-four I tried to abandon this idea, but I did so with the consciousness that I (1) <u>was outraging</u> my true nature and that sooner or later I should have to settle down and write books.

I (2) <u>was</u> the middle child of three, but there was a gap of five years on either side, and I barely (3) <u>saw</u> my father before I was eight. For this and other reasons I was somewhat lonely, and I soon (4) <u>developed</u> disagreeable mannerisms which (5) <u>made</u> me unpopular throughout my schooldays. I had the lonely child's habit of making up stories and holding conversations with imaginary persons, and I (6) <u>think</u> from the very start my literary ambitions (7) <u>were mixed</u> up with the feeling of being isolated and undervalued. I (8) <u>knew</u> that I had a facility with words and a power of facing unpleasant facts, and I felt that this created a sort of private world in which I could get my own back for my failure in everyday life. Nevertheless the volume of serious — i.e. seriously intended — writing which I produced all through my childhood and boyhood (9) <u>would</u> not <u>amount</u> to half a dozen pages. I (10) <u>wrote</u> my first poem at the age of four or five, my mother taking it down to dictation. I (11) <u>cannot</u> remember anything about it except that it was about a tiger and the tiger had 'chair-like teeth' — a good enough phrase, but I (12) <u>fancy</u> the poem was a plagiarism of Blake's 'Tiger, Tiger'. At eleven, when the war or 1914-18 (13) <u>broke</u> out, I wrote a patriotic poem which (14) <u>was printed</u> in the local newspaper, as was another, two years later, on the death of Kitchener. From time to time, when I was a bit older, I wrote bad and usually unfinished 'nature poems' in the Georgian style. I also (15) <u>attempted</u> a short story which was a ghastly failure. That was the total of the would-be serious work that I actually (16) <u>set</u> down on paper during all those years.